WELCOMING COMMITTEE

Awakened by the row, Gene started to his feet and rushed to the cave entrance. A silent machine like a chrome-plated stick-figure awaited him. It was impeccably programmed. The back of his head sank into a resilient pad and a band closed around his neck; his arms, his torso, his legs were matched from behind by clasping metal limbs with joints in precisely the right places to let him move . . . provided he did so very slowly.

Also there was the sting of a diadermic on the inside of his left elbow, on feeling which he screamed.

Because at that instant dreadful memories stormed in.

Also by John Brunner
Published by Ballantine Books:

BEDLAM PLANET

CATCH A FALLING STAR

DOUBLE, DOUBLE

THE DRAMATURGES OF YAN

THE GREAT STEAMBOAT RACE

THE INFINITIVE OF GO

THE LONG RESULT

PLAYERS AT THE GAME OF PEOPLE

THE SHEEP LOOK UP

SHOCKWAVE RIDER

STAND ON ZANZIBAR

TIMES WITHOUT NUMBER

THE WEBS OF EVERYWHERE

THE WHOLE MAN

The Tides Of Time

JOHN BRUNNER

A Del Rey Book

BALLANTINE BOOKS • NEW YORK

A Del Rey Book
Published by Ballantine Books

Copyright © 1984 by Brunner Fact & Fiction, Ltd.

Library of Congress Catalog Card Number: 84-90942

ISBN 0-345-31838-2

Printed in Canada

First Edition: December 1984

Cover Art by Don Dixon

Prologue

The night when it was over was the longest of the
year . . . and by far the longest of his life. He carried
his burden of sorrow to the forepeak of the island, where
those who had come to hold a wake with him dug a fire
pit after the ancient manner, sprinkling on seawater and
adding fragrant herbs before they covered it and lit the
wood.

They whiled away the darkest hours with songs and
tales. He did not know how to join in, nor was he invited
to.

The eastern sky grew pale. They broached a wineskin
and with ceremony circulated it to all save him. It made
no odds; he was in no mood to drink. Then silence fell,
and all eyes turned to the horizon.

When once again they'd watched the oldest miracle,
the death and rebirth of the light, they ritually shared the
meal, but offered nothing to the widower. Him they left

1

solitary with his grief—the powerless, the unfulfilled, the man whose life was incomplete, still at the mercy of more suffering.

Thus it had been in olden days. Thus it would have to be again next year.

On whatsoever planet of the cosmos.

1

THE EXHIBIT

is huge and hollow, made of metal, pitted and scarred.
It has been to somewhere that cannot exist

THE MONTH

is April

THE NAME

is Suleyman

AFTER WEEKS OF TRAVEL TO STRANGE AND UNFAMIL-
iar places—but they were adapted to that, better
than anybody, better than everybody—on a spring
evening when the air was turning from warm to chill
and the sea from blue to gray thanks to the shadow of
a thunderstorm, they came to an island which had
nearly the shape of a sphinx. Brownish, flecked with
sparse vegetation but innocent of trees, it reared
broad haunches high above the water, with beaches
on its eastern and western flanks and another, the
smallest, between two rocky outcrops that modeled
forelimbs underneath its south-turned chin.

Perhaps it had a name. Boat could not inform them
if so; like most maps, hers were out of date or
incomplete, and they had forbidden her to interro-
gate any satellites.

For a long while Gene surveyed it frowning from

her bow, stretching each of his lean dark limbs in turn.

At length he said, "I don't much like the look of it."

But that was hardly surprising. He distrusted islands. He was in the habit of insisting that his ancestors on both sides had been of continental stock—though how he, an orphan, could be certain was a mystery—and had bequeathed him the subconscious conviction that the whole universe was, or ought to be, a single landmass which a tribe could walk across. Supposedly this was what accounted for . . .

But they had a tacit bargain not to speak of such matters. Besides, Stacy's attitude was opposite to his, which meant one theory or the other must be wrong.

For the moment she was disinclined to pursue the matter, anyway. She contented herself with saying, "I think it might be advisable to land. Water's all very well while it's calm, but when the storm breaks . . ."

"I guess you're right," sighed Gene, and instructed Boat to make for shore.

Programmed to avoid habitation so far as possible, she chose the beach between the sphinx's paws, for there were traces of human activity on both the others: abandoned shacks, a caïque moored to a post now lower than its bow, in the restive water anchored nets that had trapped empty barrels, mostly of plastic but a few of wood.

And this third one was not devoid of people's leavings, either. As they drew closer, Gene and Stacy made out concrete beams, square, grayish white, patched with red and brown smears. Some still composed an archway extending the mouth of a cave in the living rock; many more were askew, their foundations eroded by the rise in water level; some lay partly buried by encroaching sand, and a few were completely submerged.

Neither of them spoke again until Boat touched bottom and extended her forward gangplank. Then, tense and nervous as ever, Gene strode to its end. He stared about him first, then upward at the overhang of the sphinx's jaw, and stood irresolute.

Following more slowly, but more composed, Stacy passed him and set foot on the nearest of the fallen columns. Its concrete was dissolving under the onslaught of salt water, assisted by borer worms and tenacious weed. Halting, she studied those of its counterparts which were still erect enough to be regarded as pillars and lintels.

Eventually she said, "It's a temple of Ares."

"Who?"

"God of war."

"Ridiculous! This is far too—"

She cut him short impatiently. "Not classical, naturally! But he's always with us . . . Boat!"

The vessel responded more readily to her than him; that had been a source of friction during their journey. "Yes, Anastasia?" she answered in her clear light voice.

"What is this place? It looks like a twentieth century strongpoint—more likely World War II than I."

"The chances are that you're correct, but I have no data on its origin."

"So much forgotten and so much to know . . ." murmured Stacy.

But she was forever saying things of that kind, and Gene paid no heed. Eyeing the impending storm, he reminded her, "You suggested we ought to take shelter."

She turned slowly through half a circle. Above her the jutting chin of the sphinx was bearded with drying rootlets hung in air: plants which had contrived to establish themselves in cracks and crevices were falling from their own excessive growth. To either side, the oblong relics of an ancient conflict recalled an age when humanity too seemed to face no greater threat to its survival than those entailed by competition with itself. The little headlands were stark and bare; the shore was narrow and much scarred with rocks; but near the entrance of the concrete archway tufts of saltgrass grew and the yellow-gray of sand changed to the brown of fertile earth.

She said at last, "You can't deny we'd be better off ashore during a gale. Indeed, this may perhaps . . ."

Her last words trailed away. Impatient, he prompted her.

"Perhaps what?"

"Be the right place." She straightened abruptly, smiling as she shook back her long hair. They had discarded clothing as soon as the climate permitted. It seemed improper to be clad on this shared journey into the unknown inasmuch as they had been obliged to set out naked on those they had undertaken separately. Now she was tanned overall, as though attempting to share his blackness. Yet they had never touched each other save by unintention . . .

Her mention of "the right place" signified nothing to him, except that she claimed to feel at home among

8

these archipelagoes. Well, this was more her heritage than his, and for tonight he could pretend to himself that they were on the seashore of a proper landmass . . . insofar as any such remained. He said gruffly, "Boat, give us what we need to put up here."

The craft did not react at once. Instead, her scanners swiveled back and forth, and the air tautened with the barely sensed hum of ultrasonics. Also there was bubbling near her stern as water was sucked in for sampling.

Meantime Stacy wandered off to examine the rusty smears on the other concrete columns. Watching her, Gene did not at first register how long the delay was growing.

Then, with a start, he saw that Boat was emitting items he would never have expected: first, digging tools and a great roll of net; then something in bags— fertilizer!

Dismayed, he realized his order had been much too general, and countermanded it. She stopped work at once.

"What's wrong?" Stacy called, glancing toward the storm. It was already close enough for them to see how it was shattering the water into jagged fragments.

Fuming, Gene forced out, "This damned boat—!"

"She's a splendid boat, and I won't hear otherwise!" Stacy cut in, striding back. The pattern made by her nipples, moving in counterpoint with her hips, registered on Gene's awareness as the graph of a hugely subtle equation. Sometimes he thought there must be something dreadfully wrong with him. Other times he was certain there must be something utterly, even terrifyingly, right, and with her too, in view of what had happened to them both . . . but he had never quite managed to work out what.

"Look!" he challenged her. "Just look!" And pointed out the way Boat's resources were being wasted on an overnight campsite.

After a thoughtful pause, however, all Stacy said was—and not to him—"Amend! Supplies for supper and breakfast, beds and toilet gear will be enough."

Boat withdrew the fertilizer, tools and nets at once, to be recycled, but she was tired, and the light she depended on to run her was fading fast. Besides, the sun was dimmer than it had been when she was built. By the time she had delivered hotbeds, food, and the rest of what Stacy had reduced the order to, the rain came sprinkling down and both of them were running with wet before they managed to take refuge under the ancient archway. Access to the cave beyond proved to be blocked by a fallen boulder, but there was plenty of shelter for them and their belongings. The beds were badly underpowered, owing to Boat's depleted energy level, but fortunately Stacy's reference to "toilet gear" had been old-fashioned enough to imply towels, and two had been produced from store in sealed bags.

As well as other necessaries, Boat had supplied a coldlight, being programmed not to overlook how much human beings prize their oldest luxury, the theft of extra waking hours from darkness. Looking for a ledge to stand it on, Gene caught sight of something brightly colored on the ground, and picked it up. Torn and stained, it proved to be an advertising leaflet for a travel agency, replete with pictures of vanished beaches and holidaymakers now long dead. He sighed and let it fall—then retrieved it, thinking it might come in handy if he had to light a fire.

By the lamp's pale glow he was examining without enthusiasm what had been issued to them as suitable provisions—mainly, a self-heating pack containing a stew of forced vegetables with rice, though at least there was also a self-chilling bottle of white wine—when Stacy said unexpectedly, "Gene, I'm not used to this, and my arms are getting tired. Could you finish drying my hair, please?"

He reacted with astonishment, for she had never asked a personal favor of him before, let alone admitted physical weakness. But he gave a shrug and complied, kneeling behind her as she tilted back her head.

Outside, the first lightning struck, and thunder rolled. It was not truly cold in their artificial cave, yet age-old instinct decreed it should have been; Gene felt a shiver tremble down his spine.

There was a certain satisfaction in rubbing the long tresses of Stacy's hair between the doubled layers of the towel. The cloth bore an aroma which no doubt was factory-implanted, yet touched another chord of memory and made him think of linen wind-dried in a garden fragrant with flowers and herbs. He fought away from the association because it was personal and superficial, inasmuch as those of his ancestors whom he chose to identify with had not been rich enough to waste ground on plants they couldn't eat or wear. Nor, come to that, would they have known flax.

Yet, though he had done his best to disown them, some of his progenitors must have been European, and they at least could have been acquainted with such things . . .

He reapplied himself to his task with vigor, and shortly Stacy pronounced herself satisfied and they turned to their meal. Meantime Boat, keeping station just offshore, tight-beamed them music of a kind she judged appropriate. In view of the region they had come to, it consisted of long and wailing lines with no fixed scale Gene could discern, although—like the scent on the towels—it gave him the annoying impression that he should have known much more about its origins. Stacy, at least, seemed to appreciate what was offered, food and sound alike.

Three hours after nightfall the storm attained such a pitch that Boat felt obliged to retreat to open water, and her music faded. They lay down in the artificial twilight, separated by the remnants of their repast, together but alone, with nothing to listen to save the rain as it pelted on the roof and traced its way toward the ground and then the sea.

It was time for Stacy to ask the inevitable question. She postponed it until he dared to hope that for once she might repress it altogether. No such luck; out it came.

"Do you think they know where we are tonight?"

The sigh he greeted the words with was near a groan, but he controlled himself.

"Sure they do. We're on a long leash, that's all."

"But in weather like this—!" She was pleading for reassurance. "Not even the newest satellites can see through storm clouds!"

"I'm convinced they still have a trace on Boat."

"We've searched her stem to stern and disabled everything we could find! . . ." But her voice trailed away. She had said that before, and every time he had simply echoed her last four words. There was too much truth in that repetition for either of them to consider arguing about it anymore. Once more she lay quiet, while Gene, lulled by the pattering rain, drifted to the edge of sleep.

Then, unprecedentedly, Stacy spoke anew.

"I can't stop thinking about poor Suleyman, you know. Why don't you tell me what became of him?"

Gene rose on one elbow and blinked at her, uncomprehending. After a pause he said, "I don't know what you mean. How could anybody do that?"

"No, no!" She too sat up, brushing aside her hair. "I want to be told—I suppose I want to be told . . . Oh, never mind. Sorry." And lay down again.

But he was fully reawakened now, thanks to mention of that name. He said obstinately, "What did you *mean*?"

"I—I don't know. And yet I think . . . Put out the light, will you? Otherwise I'll never get to sleep."

Shrugging, he made a long arm and obeyed. She spoke next time in total darkness.

"Tell me what would have been right to happen to him."

Abruptly it dawned on him what she was driving at. Nonetheless for a while longer he lay confused, sorting ideas in his mind like a meteor sweeper hunting through a thousand kilometers of tangled nets in search of a profitable catch. The rain beat down harder yet; the rushing of water grew to a crescendo, as though the universe were again about to dissolve around them. But he could accept, at this time, in this place, that it would not.

Moreover, in a sense, he had shared ancestors with Suleyman; at any rate, his and his forebears might well have been cousins in Islam, albeit their descendants had followed different paths. Therefore, to his own surprise, he found words forming patterns, which he uttered. He said, "Oh yes! I know the proper way to end *his* story.

"There was a time when he got where he was meant to go. You never met him, any more than I did, but I'm sure you know as much about him as I do. Am I nor right to view him as a person caught in conflict?"

For a second he was tempted to include, "Like you and me!"—but overcame the impulse.

"Rejecting the religion his family raised him in, with its resignation to the will of God, he must have been a most unhappy man, despite what we were told about his brilliance with computers. For anybody who's been accustomed to certainty, then robbed of it, must it not be a cruel doom to have to reinvent the destiny of mind?"

She murmured something, possibly agreement. Encouraged, he went on.

"At the end of his long journey, he found a world of quiet halls and even lights. It had no name, the place he came to, for it wasn't necessary, and there were no people either, for fragile flesh and blood were obsolete. There was still air, however, and it vibrated ceaselessly with the music of machines which, in total dedication to the principles of logic, were attempting to deduce the nature and purpose of the universe.

"As a result of Suleyman's intrusion, flaws appeared. How could a man from our discordant planet match such rhythm, such subtle harmony, elaborated

over countless centuries? For some considerable
while he wished he could run away, being afraid of
how he jarred, how his mere presence broke the even
tenor of this place.

"But the grave and wise machines he fell among—
had they been human, I could see them tall and robed
and sometimes bearded—they were aware of the existence of external worlds . . . and of the past. They
gave him food, and it was good to eat, though they
themselves absorbed raw energy. Speech, too, had
long been unnecessary to them, yet they addressed
him in courteous experimental phrases deduced from
their inspection of him and their knowledge of the
cosmos, and very soon he grew acquainted with the
fashion of things there. His manners came to match
the world he fell on; his questions no longer betrayed
his shameful ignorance. He learned, and in the
learning found fulfillment. There was after all no
grand divide between the way a flawless mechanism
worked, and the reality which had so often disappointed him. There couldn't be, if these machines had
set themselves the same task as humanity and believed they stood a better chance of arriving at their
goal."

He paused, pondering what to say next because he
was so taken aback by his own insight, and she
exclaimed, "Go on! Go on for pity's sake!"

Mustering the shreds of his imagination, he continued.

"If it could be said, it would be said that such a
place was too perfect for anybody who was—old?—
enough to recall a flawed world like our own. The end
of Suleyman's tale has to be both tragic and trium-
phant."

"Explain! Explain!"

"It must consist in recognition of his plight. It must consist in his admission that the world he came to was already doomed by his existence. Because of him, its planned perfection was deranged. No matter how he struggled to adapt, the machines would thereafter recall as actual knowledge an imperfection that had previously been theory. They were forbidden to deceive themselves."

"So sad! So sad!" she whispered, her tone verging on a sob. "The perfection sought by Suleyman, then, was—"

"It was something we cannot create, we who are creatures. It was something he had sought in vain in our creations, which are necessarily less perfect than their makers. No more was it to be found on the world he traveled to. Nor anywhere."

"Perhaps because he was searching in the wrong way?"

"Conceivably." Gene fought a yawn and lost. "But as to what the right one is, or if there is one—!"

"Is there a maker, do you think?"

"We are makers," he said stonily. "We have to be."

"Yes . . . Yes. I guess so. There's no one else. At least he found his place, as we've found ours . . . There's something wrong with this bed. Gene, let me lie with you. I'm cold. I'm very cold."

It was the first time. In the morning the weather was fine again. But there had been something magical about the storm.

2

THE EXHIBIT

is a sheet of tattered paper bearing colored pictures.
It reflects a world that has vanished forever

THE MONTH

is May

THE NAME

is Ingrid

WHEN GENE AWOKE, HE WAS ALARMED TO DIS-
cover that their rented cabin cruiser was no
longer safely beached; one of her mooring cables had
parted. But he must have made a good job of securing
the other, for there she lay bobbing in early sunlight,
sleek and white among gentle ripples. He hastened to
fetch his binoculars and inspect her right away, to see
if the storm had damaged her, but she bore no
apparent trace of the ordeal she had undergone bar
the fact that some paint had been scraped from her
cutwater and the neatly lettered name bestowed by
her mocking owner—*Fairweather Friend*—was almost illegible.

Well, so long as no harm had been sustained to her
planking . . . But he'd better make certain. Doubtless she was insured; she remained, however, their
only means of getting away from this isolated spot
without attracting attention.

Stacy was still asleep. He reached a decision. After glancing around to confirm there was no one in sight, he scrambled down the three or four rocky meters to the beach, discarded the shorts and sandals he had pulled on, and waded out to the boat. He reached her with the water only chest-high.

Leaving dripmarks all over the deck and the cabin carpet, he confirmed that they had been amazingly lucky; her hull was intact. He was humming when he reemerged from below, and looking forward to breakfast.

It was a complete shock when he heard someone hail him from close by.

Spinning around, hands reflexively flying to cover his nudity, he saw a man about his own age, with ginger hair and freckles, leaning on the after gunwale and grinning at him. He wore a red shirt and there was a diver's watch on his left arm. He stood casually balanced in a rocking rowboat, on whose after thwart sat another, much older man, face lined and swarthy above a black denim smock. Incongruously, the latter sported gold-rimmed sunglasses.

"Don't worry about your lack of pants," the freckled man said. "We've had to get used to people in the raw since tourists started to invade us. Even my father-in-law—old Stavros here—is resigned to it now, like the other locals, though I'm not so sure about our *papa* . . . I'm Milo Hamilton, by the way, and the reason I'm Greek with a Scots name goes back to a British soldier who fell in love with my grandmother and settled here because it reminded him of the Hebridean island he was born on but with better weather and better cooking." His grin grew wider than ever.

"Well—ah—come aboard!" Gene suggested, wondering how he could reach at least a towel if they accepted.

"Thanks, but no thanks; we're on an errand. We just caught sight of you and thought we'd better check that you rode out the storm okay. Since we find you in good shape, we'll be on our way. Oh, I should have said: you can buy bread and wine and stuff at Oragalia Port"—pointing in the direction of the hamlet on the eastern beach—"and there's a track across the headland if you care to make it on foot. I keep the taverna, by the way. Just ask for me if you need help."

He was about to resume his thwart and oars with the ease of one accustomed to the sea, when Gene said hastily, "Just a moment! You mentioned tourists. Uh . . . Are we likely to be bothered by them?"

Milo favored him with a sweeping glance that said, as plain as words, "Aren't you pretty much a tourist yourself?" But he kept his poise, and said aloud: "Don't know what you mean by bothered! I know what I mean by it—gangs of 'em from all the cold northern countries, not a one polite enough to learn a word of the local language, demanding the same kind of food they're used to at home, getting falling-down drunk because they find the wine so cheap here, throwing up all over my floor . . . It's too early in the season for the worst of them, though. You may find a few kids wandering this way, but all they want to do is peel off, swim and laze around. They're pretty harmless, though if I were you I'd keep an eye on my more valuable belongings. They have been known to claim the world owes them a living . . . *Endaxi, Stavro—piyainoumé!*"

Gene watched the boat depart with mixed feelings. Eventually, however, he gave a shrug and waded back to shore.

When he regained their shelter, this relic of war well above sea level which they had so providentially spotted last night with both their radio and their sonar out, Stacy was sitting up with her half of the sleeping bag clutched around her knees, her dark and long-lashed eyes ajar with worry.

"I heard you talking to someone!" she exclaimed.

Soothing, he explained. "I went to make sure the *Friend* was okay after the storm, and she is. Someone in a passing rowboat spotted her and came to find out if we were in any trouble. Nice guy—owns the local taverna. Said to call on him for anything we need."

But Stacy was still haunted by suspicion. "Are you sure?" she countered.

"Sure he owns the taverna? Well, until I see him behind the bar—"

"Stuff it, will you? You know damned well what I mean!" She scrambled out of the bag and seized her jeans and panties, drawing them on in a succession of panicky jerks, then donned a tee shirt and combed loose her sleek black hair with her fingers.

He made to embrace her, but she pushed him away. "I'm full to bursting! Is there any place I can go?"

"Try the sea," he said, turning aside with a shrug. "You needn't have worried about getting dressed, incidentally. The guy said the locals are used to people in the altogether."

"What? You mean we've found our way to—?"

"Yes, damn it! There are tourists here! Like us!"

For a moment he expected her to snap back at him; instead, she thrust her feet into her sandals and made for the entrance.

"What the hell," she said despondently. "We've screwed up this planet past hope of recovery. Any extra mess of mine won't make much difference."

"At least it's biodegradable!" he chaffed. But she had hurried out of earshot.

During her absence, he occupied himself in preparing breakfast. Their bread was stale, but still edible, and there remained a hunk of cheese and plenty of olives. Also there was enough water for coffee, so he lit their little butane stove and hunted out the rest of their stock of sugar and powdered milk.

Meantime, he was silently cursing himself. What in the world had persuaded him to accept Stacy's view that it was easier to elude pursuit among islands, where the arrival of anybody was an event, let alone a couple like themselves, than on a good solid continent with all its means of emergency escape, by air or car or train or even on foot?

Well, he was—they were—here today. And he was damned if he was going to let himself imagine, as she appeared to, a threat of discovery around every corner!

By the time Stacy returned, without having yielded to the temptation of a swim, he had sliced the bread and cheese and laid it on plastic plates, together with a twisted brown-paper cone containing the olives. She sat down facing him and ate without speaking until only a single olive remained.

"Want it?" she said then.

"You have it."

"That means you want it."

Traveling with this woman seemed to be an endless succession of such petty disputations. Right now he was relaxed enough to counter her.

"It means I'd like it. But so would you, and I don't want it enough to deprive you."

"Oh, all this over one measly olive!" she exclaimed, and picked up the oily paper as though to throw it away, and the olive with it. He caught her arm.

"Let go of me!"

"No, wait. I just had a great idea. Pass me a knife."

Which taking ceremoniously, he used to halve the wrinkled black ovoid.

Seeing it laid out, neatly dissected, on his pale palm, she bit her lip, then grinned, then laughed outright and ate her half. Afterward, growing serious again, she said, "If we're going to hide out here for a while, we'll need more provisions."

"We can buy them in Milo's village—Just a moment! Are we going to stick around? Who said we were?"

She shrugged, leaning back against the rough concrete wall of their temporary home.

"I thought you wanted me to take your word concerning this character in a rowboat who 'just happened' to spot us. Also the *Friend* is low on fuel, right?"

Gene drew a deep breath. Adjusting to these total reversals of her attitude was something he should by now have grown accustomed to, yet he still found it hard.

"Tell me," he invited cautiously, "why you think we

ought to stay here, even for a day or two, when normally you're convinced there are spies everywhere."

"Oh, yes, I know!" she flared. "You want a continent behind you! But you were raised on one which doesn't have national frontiers like mine, with passport officers and customs searches at every step you take! You don't regard islands as being real, do you? And I quote! To hell with you and your 'ancestors of continental stock!' *My* subconscious feeling of security consists in having lots of nice deep water around me, like a moat!"

Gene struggled to stay calm. He said in his mildest tone, "Fine, fine! You think it's advisable to stay here. I only asked you to spell out why."

His reasonableness confounded her for a moment. Then she said, "Anyway, I don't suppose an island like this has many phones, so rumors about our presence could take a long while to spread."

"There must be a radiophone at least—" he began.

"I said *many*! Who'd lay phone cables for a place like this? Think it's infested with highly paid reporters?"

"Well, if there's a tourist trade—" He had it in mind to beat her to the possibility of mainland newspapers circulating here, or pictures of her, if not him, being shown on TV. Mistaking his intention, she cut him short.

"Too bad if one of the visitors falls ill, or his company goes broke or what the hell! Actually"— chuckling into yet another of her swift and unpredictable changes of mood—"I can just picture what would happen. Who would he be? A Dutchman or a

Dane, most likely, a not quite successful sort of self-employed businessman, proud of the fact he speaks one foreign language and unprepared to learn a second, here with his wife and teenage children because they persuaded him that islands like this are the fashion now for holidays, but hating every moment, and suddenly overcome in the middle of the night by the conviction that he's about to lose a million gulden. Or whatever."

The detail of her vision was infectious; it reminded Gene of the story she'd insisted on him telling her about—Whom had it been about? An old friend, or someone who had not exactly been a friend . . . He strove to recapture it. But it proved elusive as a dream.

Maybe that was what it had been. Certainly its essence seemed unreal in the sober light of morning. He applied himself to elaborating her brief fantasy, saying, "Why, yes, of course! He'd go to the post office—if they have such a thing here—and he'd make himself misunderstood in his two wrong languages and he'd get more and more panicky, and eventually his son, or better his daughter, who'd have struck up an acquaintance with one of the locals, would come to him and say soothingly, 'Dad, they only have telephone service on Mondays and Fridays, so why don't you sit on the beach with us till then?' And—"

But she had lost interest, rousing herself to collect their plates and the few crusts of bread they had left.

"Are there any seagulls I can throw the scraps to?"

"No gulls," he said. He remembered that distinctly. "Or other birds?"

"I didn't see any," he admitted, and for some reason felt uncomfortable.

"I'll bury them, then. The ground looks as though it could do with a bit of humus. Let's go and buy more food and wine, and fill the water bottle. Then we can spend a lazy day by ourselves, swimming and lying in the sun."

"We may not be alone," Gene muttered, and repeated what Milo had said.

"Well—so? The world belongs to all of us."

Half an hour ago she had seemed terrified by his chance encounter with Milo. Now she appeared to have forgotten all about the risk of their being recognized. Her mind must be spinning like a weathervane. Resignedly, Gene hauled himself to his feet.

"That's as may be! But there are lots of things aboard the *Friend* which we have no right to redistribute to strangers! I'll make her secure. Back in a minute!"

When he returned she was naked again, except for panties, and kneeling in front of the bag of clothes she had brought ashore, pondering what to change into. This, he knew, was a process not to be interrupted. Waiting patiently, he noticed things on the ground which had not been there earlier: five or six tarnished brass shell cases, probably spent by an automatic rifle.

"Where did these come from?" he inquired curiously.

"Oh, I found them while I was burying the rubbish. The beach is littered with them, just below the surface . . . Will this do, do you think?" She rose, holding up before her a beige linen minidress.

"Perfectly," he said. "But then you know my view: you look gorgeous in anything, or nothing. Especially nothing."

She pulled a face at him and drew the exiguous garment over her head; it reached barely halfway down her thighs. Thrusting her feet into sandals, and picking up a woven reed bag to hold their purchases, she invited him with a gesture to lead her to the path across the headland which Milo had pointed out. In burning heat, although the sun was less than halfway to the zenith, they picked their way among pebbles washed bare by last night's rain, slipping occasionally on mud not yet dried out. The low sharp branches of surrounding shrubs attacked their calves, and insects buzzed in search of the rare blue flowers, and still one thing was missing. Stacy said at last, when they paused for breath at the crest of the track, "You're right. There are no birds."

"No. Just us."

"*Not* just us," she contradicted, pointing. The path at this point followed a cliff edge, and had brought them into sight of a handsome yacht, no doubt heading toward the little port for which they too were bound, with ten or a dozen passengers gathered along her rail, and several crew. At such a distance it was impossible to discern what flag she flew; fortunately, Stacy was too preoccupied to worry about her provenance.

"An island having people, that lacks birds . . ." She gazed down, shielding her eyes against the sun.

"They made the wrong choice."

"What do you mean?" She drew back and stared at him.

"Birds. That was the way the reptiles chose—the dinosaurs. They could have been intelligent, like us. I saw it on TV. Instead they decided on another course. They took to the air. And we *over*took them." Gene gave a forced laugh to show he wasn't altogether serious.

But she accepted his words at their face value. Sounding troubled, she said, "You mean the world's resources could have been exhausted long ago, if something hadn't happened to prevent the dinosaurs from digging coal."

Taken by her fancy, as in the case of the imaginary pompous Dutchman, Gene nodded.

"Or drilling for oil, mining uranium, and come to that launching into space. We aren't so special; it might have happened long ago."

"Then what would this island have been like? Would it have been here at all?" Turning, she surveyed it; from here they could not see it whole by any means, but this eastern side was webbed with rocky ridges and notched to form little sandy inlets. All but one of those in view were specked with tents like multicolored fungi: spaced far apart as yet, but presaging a later richer crop.

"Ask a geologist; I'm not one. Shall we move on?"

"Yes, I guess so . . ." She handed him the bag, which, even empty, was a burden in this heat, and scrambled onward down the narrow path.

Shortly they reached the village, and found the yacht had cast anchor in its bay and discharged its passengers. There were too few of them to constitute a crowd, yet they gave the impression of an invading horde. They were not in competition with Gene and

Stacy as they went about their business of buying bread, fish and fruit, tomatoes and wine and oil, enough to last the day, but complained loudly about the lack of souvenir shops and the difficulty of finding good vantage points to take a photo from. Their cameras reawakened Stacy's fears and made her reluctant to consider Gene's suggestion of a drink at the taverna before returning, though both were thirsty.

"Suppose—!" she whispered.

"Suppose what? One of this lot is a *paparazzo* with a line to the Italian scandal sheets? Out of the question! Besides, in a place like this it's worth being on good terms with the guy who runs the bar. And you did say you fancied the idea of staying here for a while."

"Oh, all right. I'm not ashamed of what we've done."

Ashamed? Well, maybe not. Terrified, though, half the time at least . . . Gene put his arm around her and felt her trembling. But there was no help for that.

The taverna was not hard to locate, for apart from the little church it was the largest soundest building; most of the others were tumbledown or ramshackle. Before they reached it, however, it was beset by the yacht's passengers, shouting orders—none of them in Greek—and complaining about the slowness of the service.

But Gene was sufficiently out of the ordinary for Milo to pay them special attention when they sat down. Passing with a grimace, he muttered, "The season's started early—maybe with you! I should have known! Wine and *mezedes*? On the way!" And to someone else: "*Oriste*—coming!"

Stacy touched her companion's arm. "Gene, I think we ought to get away from here!" she whispered.

"Nonsense!" he answered bluffly. "Who'd expect to find the *famous* Anastasia and the *notorious* Eugene—?"

"Everybody's looking at us!" she countered.

"Okay, why not? I mean, I'm black and you're beautiful! And you are, damn it! You're gorgeous!"

His attempt to distract her with compliments failed.

"Gene! That man over there has a newspaper!"

"Are we headline news in it? Stacy, it's been weeks! You know a story like ours doesn't last that long!" He leaned toward her, hoping to keep their dispute quiet enough not to attract attention. At once her face hardened and her voice acquired a shrill edge.

"You don't understand! All you're concerned about is that you've made off with an heiress!"

"I didn't think that was the way of it!" he snapped.

"It wasn't meant to be! At first I believed . . . The hell with it. Let's go." She jumped to her feet.

"Well, if you're determined to create a scene—"

"Determined? Hell, no, I was hoping for something absolutely different! But it's up to you, after all. Come along, and don't leave the bag behind!"

Providentially, at that instant Milo dumped a carafe of retsina on their table, along with glasses and a saucerful of goat's cheese and olives. Making a logical assumption, he addressed Stacy.

"If you're looking for what I think you are, it's back that way—there's a sign. Unisex, I'm afraid, but it was empty a moment ago."

She hesitated. Then, with vast effort, she controlled herself and nodded. As she departed Gene heaved a giant sigh of relief. For in a sense she was right. How could a mixed-race couple hope to remain inconspicuous in a village like this? But before he could calm her enough to lure her back to the sort of place where he felt safe, the middle of a good solid continent, he was going to have to allay her sense of paranoia. And the problem there was that it had a basis in reality: her grandfather—her *adoptive* grandfather—probably was ruthless enough to hire thugs to beat him up and drag her home.

On the other hand, she *had* begged to be taken away from the only world she had ever known; she *had* pleaded for a chance to live another existence than that of the jet set; she *had* decided that he was the right person to try it with; she *had* arranged all those misleading clues which ought to indicate that she had fled to South America . . . and, judging from the few newspapers they had risked buying, the bait had been swallowed by the press, at least. No, the odds were still in their favor—though it was a damned nuisance about this yachtload of sightseers.

Stacy was calmer when she returned, and they drank their wine more or less at leisure amid the clamorous and never-ceasing shouts of the other foreign customers. But when they reached the last glassful she began to fidget again, and he too was glad to pay up and leave, conscious of how many eyes were on them and worried as to what Stacy was apt to do or say next: insist on packing up and moving on?

To his amazement, however, even before they had regained the trail over the headland, she suddenly linked fingers with him and gave a squeeze.

"Gene, weren't they awful—those people?"

"Well, this morning Milo said . . ." And he para-phrased as best he could, adding a couple of caustic extra comments.

"I used to be like them." She was staring straight ahead up the steep path. "I don't want to be like them anymore. Though I couldn't help it. It was the way I was brought up. You do know that, don't you?" She turned to him with a beseeching expression.

"Yes, I do," he answered gruffly. "Otherwise I wouldn't be here, would I?"

"That's all right then. So long as we're together, everything is all right, isn't it?"

And, leaving him to follow more slowly with the bag of provisions, she almost danced to the top of the hill.

When they arrived back at "their" beach, however, they found it occupied by strangers: a boy and girl both about twenty, she stretched out nude on a towel while he—equally unclad—anointed her back with suntan oil. They looked up curiously, and the boy addressed them in rudimentary Greek. At their baffled response he switched first to sketchy German, then to English, and got through.

"That's your stuff there in the—uh—war memo-rial?"

"Yes!" Gene advanced the last few paces, while Stacy hung back.

"Your boat, too?"

"Not exactly. Rented."

"Ah-hah. Staying long?"

"Haven't decided yet."

"That's the way," the boy said admiringly. "Cut

loose from your roots, explore the world before it's blown to bits. Wish we could do the same, but you need bread to keep going, and . . . I'm Hank. This is Linda."

The girl rose on her elbows and smiled. She was fair and pretty, but rather fat.

"Say—uh—you don't mind us? . . ." Hank made a vague gesture.

"The world belongs to all of us," Gene said, consciously quoting Stacy.

"That's good," the boy approved. "We just mean to stick around awhile and soak up some sun, that's all."

"So do we," said Stacy, having made up her mind, and stepped to Gene's side. "I'm Stacy and he's Gene, by the way. And I'm just about to fix lunch. Are you hungry?"

"Well, we got some bread and cheese and fruit—"

"So've we. Let's pool it, then." Stacy debated with herself a second, then caught up the hem of her dress and tugged it over her head. Another moment, and she discarded her bikini panties too.

"Provided," she went on, "you lend me some of that suntan oil."

It proved to be a strange day. Gene would not have thought it possible to talk so much without actually saying anything. Miraculously, however, Hank and Linda were not in the least interested in their companions' background, and spoke very little about their own. Mainly they concentrated on their view of life, which was frankly mystical. They were planning to bum their way via Turkey into India and thence to Nepal, in hopes of meeting a guru who would offer them enlightenment. Gene felt a stir of envy at their optimism. He couldn't help wondering whether this anonymous island was on their best route, but held his peace. At one stage Linda inquired diffidently whether there was any pot around, "like maybe on the boat," but accepted Gene's headshake and changed the subject.

Toward sundown the young couple resumed their clothes and headed back toward Oragalia, where they were to meet someone who might have room in a boat making for the next island in the chain. They embraced Gene and Stacy effusively but offered no thanks for the food they had shared.

When they had gone, Stacy reentered the cave by way of its concrete arch—still surprisingly true and square despite the passage of time—and set about preparing red mullet for supper. She was not a good cook, even a camp cook, but she insisted on undertaking the menial chores to prove she was capable of them.

Musingly she said, "I think if everyone were more like those two than the tourists we saw this morning the world would be a far better place. Don't you agree?"

Gene suppressed his private reservations. He said, "At least they seem very relaxed. And sort of gentle."

"Yes, gentle's a good term. Isn't there another bottle?"

Somewhat guiltily, they had concealed the last of their wine, because the sun had lain hot on the beach despite it being only May, and both Hank and Linda had displayed a colossal thirst. While Gene was drawing the cork she went on, "I can't help thinking how much Ingrid would have disliked them, and how much more like she must have been to those appalling tourists."

"Really? How do you mean?" He filled their glasses.

"Oh—" She gestured with the knife she had used to clean the fish. "It's the 'boss for a day' bit, if you see what I mean. Probably most of those people will go home to dreadful jobs where they have to kowtow all the time to the managing director or the owner or whatever, but while they're here they give orders and dish out lavish tips and everybody runs to obey them. Ingrid must have enjoyed that sort of thing. You never met her, did you?"

"No. Though I heard about her, naturally."

"Well, nor did I, but I got this very clear picture of her." Laying by the knife, she took her glass and sat down on her side of the sleeping bag, not looking at him—not looking at anything in the here and now, but blankly at the wall of the cave.

"And I've been wondering about the fate that would have been appropriate for her. Like to hear what I think?"

"Yes, of course." He too sat down, linking his fingers around his knees.

"Well, I suspect she'd have wanted to find her way to a place full of little people she could lord it over, heirs perhaps to a decadent civilization. Maybe little *brown* people—Gene, I'm sorry!"

"Nothing to do with me. Go on."

She was frowning. "Well, I think she'd have liked to be made welcome by their king, you know. Set on a throne and draped with garlands, brought offerings of meat and butter and rice. But eventually life in Lamagu would have begun to bore her . . . Funny! It's almost as though the place I'm talking about could really exist. I didn't mean to call it Lamagu, but that's its name. I mean, it feels like its name."

"Go *on*," he urged, reaching for the wine again.

"Well, like I say, she grew bored, not even needing to issue orders, but having everything done for her without asking. It wasn't enough to rise every morning and see the dawn break over distant snowcapped mountains, watch the lilies on the ornamental ponds open to greet the day, enjoy countless dishes full of unfamiliar tidbits, put on the richest silks and jewels and set forth across the city to view wild animals or listen to the music of a temple ceremony. It wasn't enough. She needed to tell someone what to do and watch it done.

"So one morning she started countermanding everything that was done for her, as a matter of routine. She found fault with no matter what— demanded that the cook bring her impossible delights for breakfast, ordered the tailor to remake her gowns, called for minstrels and decided to instruct them in her favorite hymn tune. Also she mocked them for not knowing it already, and for being ignorant of the religion her family had brought her up in, to which she only paid attention when it suited her.

"Then, later, on the streets of Lamagu, along the broad avenues where the merchants haggled with their customers and in the alleys where the tinsmiths and the cordwainers plied their trade in tiny open-fronted shops above which people slept—in rooms when it was cool, on rattan beds, or on the roofs when it was hot and there was no hope of rain for months to come—everywhere she picked on passersby at random and upbraided them for being as they were. She ordered them to change their style of dress, their diet, their homes and even their ancientest traditions.

"All this the folk of Lamagu accepted. Nor did they just accept; they welcomed it. They had been bored so long, they'd grown resigned to permanent monotony. They thought her mad, of course, but it was a fascinating kind of madness. Without her having to demand it of him, their king removed the necklace which was his mark of office, like a crown, and begged her on his bended knee to don it.

"Which she did, already half-aware that this itself had undermined her plan.

"What could she change now in the city, radically? Well, there was a problem concerning water. There was either not enough, in summer, or too much, when the rainy season came. Accordingly she decreed the building of vast reservoirs, linked by canals, with here and there a gentle waterfall and steps alongside where a family might come to fill their pots and jars. This, now, the people understood; not only was it practical, but it would provide by night the soothing music of cascading water, to replace the churr of crickets kept in cages, which had been customary but which she had now forbidden. They set to with a will, and very shortly the system was complete.

"And other droning insects came to make music in the night, well to the people's taste, for they'd had droning instruments in the temples she converted to museums.

"After the rainy season, when the reservoirs operated perfectly and stored, high in the hills, enough to meet the city's needs for the longest and hottest summer—so she was pleased—the people suddenly began to act as she had long desired. They came to her begging to be told what they should do. Delighted at this reversal of the situation she had rebelled against, she issued orders and more orders, and more and more orders, and they went away and she sat happily on the throne which had been the king's and waited for reports on the impact she had made.

"None came, but one of the new droning insects bit her ankle, and she swatted it.

"Then, at last, after sundown, she went out to see why she was being left alone, without food or drink or attendants, and found that Lamagu was full of corpses. And not long after, she was one of them."

Stacy shook herself, seeming to return from far away, and glanced around. Gene had lighted their little butane stove, and also their lamp, and was holding out a plate on which lay a fried fish appetizingly scented with wild thyme, a wedge of bread, and sliced tomatoes dressed with lemon, oil and salt.

"I was going to fix that—" she began, then meekly took it, and began to eat.

After a little she said, "Were you listening?"

"I promise you, I didn't miss a word. Eat up. It's late, and growing cold."

Soon after, twining against him in the darkness, she remembered one more thing she'd meant to say.

THE TIDES OF TIME

"You don't think Hank and Linda recognized us, do you?"

"I doubt it very much. Did they sound as though they pay attention to the news?"

"No, I guess not. But may they not be talking of us to their friends?"

"Very likely. If their friends are like them, though, we have nothing to worry about."

"Yes, you're right . . . Gene, I think I'm a little happy here. Let's stay awhile."

Dismissing all his reservations, he replied, "Okay!"

Wondering meantime when he'd regret it.

3

THE EXHIBIT

is a handful of shell cases from an automatic rifle.
They speak of a bad habit long forgotten: war

THE MONTH

is June

THE NAME

is Cedric

THE THIRTY-METER LENGTH OF *RÄUMBOOT R34*—
gray as the gray of the sea in the predawn light of
this fine June morning—plowed northward at her
steady cruising speed of 18 k.p.h. Nervous beside her
twin antiaircraft guns, her duty deck-crew yawned
and cursed their inability to dominate fatigue by an
act of will. But she was far from any battle zone now,
although a few planes had droned by during the hours
of darkness.

Sore-eyed, at the limit of the endurance bestowed
on him by coffee and Benzedrine, Leutnant Kreutzer
surveyed the island they were approaching and
identified it by the chart spread out before him on the
map table of the cramped bridge. Its name, apparently, was Oragalia. He checked his watch and made a
note in the log.

Then a familiar but unwelcome voice spoke behind
him, and Graumann appropriated his binoculars

without permission—Graumann, who was so proud of his entitlement to one of the countless uniforms invented not by the Navy but by the Party, with its incomprehensible badges of rank, who made so great a point of dragging his right leg and such a habit of referring to his "wound from the Great War." In his invariable self-important manner, he said, "That looks interesting. Where are we on the chart? . . . Ah, you've marked it"—in the tone of one disappointed at not being able to complain that the chore had been neglected. "Kindly heave to for a while and let me look it over."

Kreutzer bit back the words that sprang to his tonguetip and wearily signed to his *Bootsmann*, who had the wheel. The rumble of their twin diesels receded to a faint thump-thumping as the sun peered over the skyline and color flooded back into the world.

"Hmm!" Graumann pronounced after half a minute or so. "That southern bay has possibilities. Take the glasses, *Herr Leutnant*, and see if you can fault me on this. Suppose we were to post a lookout station on that overhang, preferably including a radar unit?" He paused to let his grasp of current technical jargon make an impression. "Then we could fortify the entrance to that cave, which could be used as a magazine—if it's big enough, and if not we'll enlarge it—site a couple of gun posts on those headlands and draft some of the local people to build a rampart of boulders blocking access from the beach: would that not strike you as a highly defensible vantage point?"

Kreutzer cursed the man silently. He could in fact not fault the argument; the chart confirmed that an outpost on Oragalia would indeed control the approaches to this corner of what had just become the latest acquisition of the Third Reich.

Such land-centered thinking, though, was foreign to him. He liked open water better, searching and chasing across a quarter of the globe if necessary. He had hoped to be posted to a U-boat pack. But each man within the Reich must do his duty, and according to its complex system of interlinked authority Graumann was his superior. He contained himself, and said only, "If the enemy does manage to regroup, which is unlikely, then he might well organize a counterattack in this area. I must say, however . . ."

"What?" Graumann was instantly affronted.

"Well, after our success in Crete, he might be tempted to imitate our example, in which case shore defenses—"

"We have air superiority throughout this region! Not a chance!" Graumann turned to the bosun. "I notice a shack on that beach, and what looks like a vegetable patch. That implies a larger community nearby, and from the map I deduce it's on the eastern shore. Send a signal to say that's where we're making for. We'll land, and give the locals a chance to get acquainted with their new masters."

"Aye, aye, sir," the bosun grunted, and called for half ahead. As the diesels resumed their former pace, Graumann turned back to the ship's commander.

"It must be a remarkable experience, *Herr Leutnant*, to arrive as the rightful conqueror of a decadent folk, which is what we are about to do. Prepare to lodge in memory what may well be a unique event for both of us. The rate at which the Reich is expanding implies that it will not often be repeated, and certainly not beyond our own lifetimes, unless in outer space. Don't you agree?"

"Evgenos! Evgenos! Wake up!"

The folk of Oragalia resented the dark-skinned stranger, because the adopted daughter of the island's richest family had chosen him in preference to any of her other suitors, rejecting her old comfortable life for an existence like the humblest peasants', with a shack for shelter, a cave to store their few tools and provisions such as flour, oil and dried fish, and a tiny patch of salty ground to scratch their living from. The men of the island, particularly her foster father, had had other plans for her. However, because when Greece was invaded so many of the fit young men had been summoned to die in places with unfamiliar names, the boat owners had lately begun to call on Evgenos for help by night . . . and pay him well. Strong arms for hauling in the net lines were too valuable to waste. This morning he had gone to sleep at cockcrow. Now here he was being roused, it seemed, almost before he had dozed off.

Cursing, he opened his eyes, and discovered that it was in fact broad daylight. Under the slanting roof of the hut he had constructed out of scrap and flotsam when challenged to prove he could support her, Anastasia was shaking him by the shoulders.

"What's the matter?" he demanded, sitting up on the rough pallet. He had been so exhausted when he came home, he had lain down in all his clothes except his boots.

"A warship has arrived off the port, a German

warship twice as big as Kaloyiannis's caïque! They've sent a landing party. They have rifles and machine guns. Everybody has been told to assemble in the square at noon!"

Completely alert now, Evgenos scrambled to his feet, rubbing his eyes, judging the time as late morning by the angle of the shadows beyond the unsquare door. "Have you seen the ship yourself?" he demanded.

"No, Xanthe came to warn me"—meaning her foster sister, whose husband had reported to his army unit months ago and not been heard from since, and with whom she had contrived to get back on good terms despite the resentment of the rest of the family which had taken her in when she was orphaned. "But it's fearful news! I'm scared!"

"Haven't we been expecting something of the kind ever since the fall of Crete? And it could have been worse. We might have been shelled, or bombed from the air."

"How can you talk like that?" Anastasia cried.

"Because it's no good talking any other way. Besides, there can't be much here that they want. This is a very poor island compared with some."

She hesitated, eyes downcast.

"They might want our land," she said at length.

"What do you mean?"

"My uncle says this bay could make a strongpoint. He says our own army should have fortified it. You've heard him go on about it often enough, haven't you?"

"Oh, him!" Her uncle-by-courtesy Rhodakis was their ex-policeman, called out of retirement when his successor was ordered to rejoin his regiment, given to holding forth on subjects he knew next to nothing about. "In that case, we certainly would have been bombed and shelled! Get me a drink of water, please, and something to quiet my belly. It's rumbling so much I can't hear myself think."

Silently she brought the water, in a large, sand-scratched, but still sound glass preserving jar which they had found when digging land for their scanty crops, and a crust of bread moistened with olive oil. Watching as he ate, she ventured, "We should hurry if we're to be in the square by noon."

"Go on ahead. And don't look for me there."

"But everybody has to—"

"What everybody has to do," he interrupted, "is find out what their plans are, and lay plans of our own to frustrate them!"

"Evgenos, you mustn't say such things!"

"Your government's been beaten! All right! Do your people want it to stay beaten forever? There are still other countries fighting against the Germans. The war isn't over by a long way!"

"It is for us!"

"For your spineless family, maybe. Not for me!"

"But even if you hide, they're bound to catch you, and then they'll punish you, and—what will become of me?"

Turning to set aside the empty cup, he shrugged. "Would you really have preferred someone who refuses to stand up against foreign invaders? You could have had your pick of men like that. But you chose me."

She caught his hand, gazing straight into his eyes. "I know," she said. "And you chose me. But it's no longer a matter of just you and me."

For a second he didn't grasp her meaning. Then his face fell. Realizing he had caught on, she nodded gravely.

"It's certain now. I'm carrying your child."

There was a moment of silence. At last, his expression grim, he said, "All the more reason to resist. Do you want him to grow up in a world where he'll be taught that he's no better than an animal? That's what the Nazis will say, you know. They'll treat him like a mongrel dog."

"But what can we possibly do against soldiers with machine guns, let alone a warship?"

"Something! Even if it's only making sure they never have a sound night's rest as long as they're here. Now run along to the village. If anyone asks where I am, say you don't know—say I couldn't sleep and went out early, or anything. But remember what I said: *don't look for me!*"

"If you're not around, someone who hates us is certain to inform on you—"

"I didn't say I wouldn't be around," he answered in a wry tone. "I just said don't look for me. Now go!"

Embracing her briefly, he strode to make a hasty toilet at the edge of the sea.

"You have nothing to fear from our garrisoning of this island! In general, you will be allowed to continue with your ordinary work, although under better administration!"

Sullenly, but on time, the citizens had gathered in the town square, facing the miniature port, with the church on one hand and the taverna on the other.

"Naturally, refusal to obey our instructions will be regarded as treason!"

Kreutzer had assigned ten of his thirty-strong crew to ring the area with rifles and submachine guns, but such precautions seemed superfluous, for these people had the air of cowed dogs. There was a flagpole on the crude mole which sheltered Oragalia's solitary harbor, used mainly to fly storm warnings; now from it fluttered the *R34*'s spare ensign, a black cross on white with the swastika at its center, the formal symbol of conquest.

And the islanders had duly obeyed Graumann's command to stand to attention, hats off, while it was hoisted. Maybe there was something to the theory of the Master Race, after all. Kreutzer himself had never enjoyed such a sense of dominance . . . but perhaps that was because he was a seaman, and the sea had never been totally tamed.

Graumann, however, was in his element, and had spent the morning interrogating these new subjects of the Reich.

In Greek, the language he was speaking now.

"Treason in a double sense, moreover—a betrayal also of your glorious Aryan heritage, the heritage which has inspired me to study your language and your culture!"

Here was another thorn in Kreutzer's flesh, for he had to appeal to his oldest and lowliest sailor for a translation: as dedicated a racialist as Graumann, and as firm a believer in the German renaissance, which he associated with the German origins of the modern Greek royal family, to the point that although his birth in Thessaloniki disqualified him from promotion even to petty officer, he had willingly transferred from the Merchant Marine at the outbreak of war. He was able to give a fair rendering of the speech, though he admitted it was so salted with classical archaicisms that now and then he had to guess at what was meant.

But Kreutzer had small trouble filling in the gaps.

"Unfortunately, with the passage of the centuries, the Nordic blood of your ancestors has become tainted, especially by Jews and other Semitic half-men! But steps will be taken to repurify all the population strains now under the protection of the Reich!"

One tall, fine-looking, but apparently frightened young woman, standing rather apart from the crowd, reacted to this last remark with a visible shudder, while a group of older people, much closer to Graumann and his companions, exchanged grave looks and nods. Kreutzer's senses were alerted, and he started to pay serious attention.

"On that subject, I've been told that some kind of blackamoor settled among you recently. I don't know who he is or what brought him here, but I notice he's conspicuous by his absence. I'm advised that he's not popular, and that few of you care to associate with him—bar one disgraceful exception!"

Kreutzer wondered whether Graumann could be referring to the young woman he had already noticed. From her tense expression and the glances cast at her from all sides, it seemed probable, although surprising. He foresaw trouble. He could guess only too clearly how his sailors might react to the presence of a woman shameless enough to give herself to a negro.

"Therefore I will accept, this once, an assurance that no one told him about this meeting. There will be another tomorrow at the same time. If he is not present then, an example will be made of his—ah—consort. That is all for the moment, but this afternoon

I propose to make a complete inspection of the island, and I shall require a guide. Arrange it."

The crowd started to disperse, and Graumann turned to Kreutzer with a thin smile.

"I think they got the message, don't you?" he murmured.

"I'm sure they did," answered the lieutenant absently, looking for the young woman. Somehow, though, she had contrived to disappear.

If he had had a gun, or even a bow and arrow, Evgenos could—and cheerfully would—have shot Graumann during his speech. One wall of the church was formed of the living rock, and it was possible to scramble up to its roof among concealing scrub for a vantage point overlooking the square. By straining his ears, he had heard everything. Now, crawling away, he was desperately wondering how to live up to his earlier boasts about resistance. It was no use worrying about the person who had informed on him; there were a score or more of candidates.

But was there anyone who might feel ashamed that that had happened? Conceivably, Kaloyiannis, who owned the largest fishing boat and had been the first to hire Evgenos as crew. He had hoped to see his own son marry Anastasia, so there was no love lost between the two of them, but he was a fiercer and sounder patriot than garrulous old Rhodakis. If the islanders were truly to be allowed to carry on with their normal work, then the fishermen would put out tonight as usual. Probably their caïques would be searched before departure, but there were too many of them for the enemy to keep them all under surveillance all night; besides, they could argue that the sound of diesel engines would scare the fish. Then suppose that a desperate man with a knife at the helmsman's throat were to order him to call at the southern tip of the island, collect Anastasia, set course for—where? Oh, anywhere! Malta, possibly, or Alexandria, though the voyage to either would be long and dangerous. At all events, it must be tried!

"So this is where the nigger and his woman live," said Graumann, uprooting with the toe of a dusty boot one of the ill-doing tomato plants that stood in a row before the shack. "How appropriate. Like the animals they are."

He turned to survey the seaward view.

"Just as I thought: an excellent spot for our permanent garrison. Don't you agree, *Herr Leutnant*?"

Sweating, thirsty, footsore, but unwilling to show any sign of weakness in Graumann's presence, Kreutzer nodded. "Though the rock is less fractured than one might have expected. Your rampart of boulders might call for quite extensive blasting."

Graumann waved that aside. "A minor matter! We can send for a shipload of concrete, and either cast it on the spot or have pillars brought in prefabricated. But this will certainly be the highlight of my next report."

"I suppose I should post guards here in case the black man comes back."

"Oh, yes. Make one of them that fellow who speaks Greek. And I want a lure staked out. Track down his woman and make sure she's here by sundown. Let it be known that she has neither food nor water. While on the subject of food, we might as well commandeer the supplies up in that cave. They're probably of dreadful quality, but every little helps."

Anastasia sat rocking back and forth in the dark, dry-eyed because she would not give her captors the satisfaction of hearing her weep. There were two: one thickset, about fifty, graying and much lined, the other half his age. The former had a pistol and the other some sort of machine gun, such as she had only seen before in pictures.

They had neither tied nor gagged her. Perhaps they hoped that if she tried to warn off Evgenos by screaming, that would make him still more likely to come to the trap for which she was the bait. They were lying out in the open atop the twin headlands, one covering the trail from the village and the other the beach. They both seemed quite calm, as though their prey were indeed an animal instead of a human being.

Well, that was what they believed, just as Evgenos had warned. Now she had heard the truth for herself. She pressed her hand to her belly, as yet barely starting to swell with the new life it bore, and suppressed a groan of despair at the fate in store for her firstborn.

Was that a noise outside? She was on her feet before she could stop herself. For a moment she stood trembling. When she had half convinced herself she was imagining things, she heard a voice at the edge of audibility . . . and recognized whose it was.

"Good evening! Aren't you the sailor who speaks Greek? Yes? It must be dull for you out here. All your friends are busy inspecting the fishing boats before they put to sea. There's no sign of the black man, by the way—he's keeping well out of sight, I'm sure, because he knows how glad we'll be to see the back of him, the bastard! Look, I brought a bottle of wine. Wouldn't you like a drop?"

There came a whispered answer, too faint to make out. Anastasia bit her lip and clenched her fists so hard the nails dug hurtfully into her palms.

"Oh, go on! Call your pal over! The nigger won't dare show himself. I bet he doesn't care enough about the woman to risk one of your bullets through his hide!"

A pause; then a reluctant word of thanks, and the Greek-turned-German sailor translated to his companion in a soft voice. In a moment there were eager scrambling noises.

What in the name of the Almighty was going on?

The guards each carried a powerful flashlight, and she was terribly afraid they might use them. But they abode by their instructions well enough not to, and all three men came together in the dark.

"Here, you first! You're a fellow countryman, after all!"

And, about as long after as it would take to raise a bottle to one's lips: a smash of glass, a cry, a thud, and the sound of a violent struggle. Anastasia could control herself no longer. She rushed out of the hut.

On rocks below the eastward headland lay the elderly ex-Greek, groaning from the pain of his fall. Up above, two men were fighting, one trying to bring his gun to bear, his opponent clutching him in a desperate wrestler's hug—and in the dimness both their faces showed pale.

She cried out in amazement. It was right. The German was distracted for a precious fraction of a second. Evgenos let go his grip, falling back and sweeping one leg around. Caught by surprise, the younger guard fell beside his companion. Evgenos jumped after him, landing on his chest with feet together. He uttered a gurgling sound and blood burst darkly from his nose and mouth.

The winner wasted no time. He kept his balance, drew a knife, and stabbed both his victims in the throat.

"Anastasia, are you all right?" he panted. "If they hurt you, I'll be sorry they enjoyed such a quick death!"

"Y-yes!" she forced out.

"Then help me drag them to the water and set them afloat! We can cover up the traces afterward!"

"How did—did you? . . ." The words wouldn't come.

He looked at her directly. Even now she almost failed to recognize him.

"How did I get to be white? I painted myself with Xanthe's Sunday makeup. Since they were looking for a black man—Or did you want to know who helped me? It was Kaloyiannis. I was pretty sure he'd swallow his dislike of me long enough to feel ashamed of the easy time the Germans are having in their occupation of the islands. He's promised to bring his caïque around and pick us up as soon as he can. But we need to dispose of this lot first."

When the job was done, they hid, wet and shivering, not in the hut or the cave, but among scrub on the higher ground, where they could keep watch both for the boat and for any sign of a patrol coming to check on the trap. But there was small risk of that; Graumann would not want his quarry frightened off.

Then, at long last, with her head on the shoulder of this violent stranger whom she seemed not to know at all even after he wiped off his pale disguise—to make him harder to spot in the dark, he explained wryly— Anastasia broke down. He waited out her dry, gusty sobs.

Eventually, as he had sometimes done in the past around the time she first decided she wanted him and no one else but was still terrified of the way she would be treated by her foster family and their friends, he decided to distract her by telling her a story.

"You know, these invaders make me think of Cedric."

"What?" She turned but did not raise her head.

"He was not just intellectual, but brilliant. He'd been an infant prodigy and grown used to adulation. Give him an IQ test and he'd finish it early and walk out before time, saying he was bored. He got to university two full years before the rest of his contemporaries, expecting he was going to blow everybody's mind there, as well.

"Didn't quite work out like that. Yes, he was bright—but so was everybody else, and some of them had experience and knowledge that he lacked. He was no longer special.

"He brooded over this, his first great disappointment, and gradually became embittered.

"Eventually his subconscious led him to a conclusion which he never voiced. He recalled how throughout his childhood his parents had promised that the world would be his oyster, and he began to believe that he'd betrayed them. Of course, they'd assured him that everything he learned was right, that everything he found in books was right, that

knowledge was his right, in other words . . . that's
total knowledge.

"From which he deduced that if by the age of
twenty-five he hadn't yet become world-famous—as,
surely, someone with his talent ought to be—there
must be a reason. At first he imagined that he had
rivals in the university, or in his field of research, who
were slandering him behind his back, or otherwise
plotting against him, but he could find no proof of
that, and he was honest enough to admit it. In the
end, all by himself, he reinvented the idea of having
been ill-wished. I suppose you know that's a standard
concept in the theory of magic. But he extended it.
He grew suspicious of the cosmos."

"Ah, but you said he never spoke of the idea!" She
lifted her head at last.

"That's right. He was afraid of mockery. So when he
set out on his journey he sought a place where what
he had to keep secret, back at home, was taken for
granted."

"Did he find it?"—sleepily.

"Yes, of course. In this infinite universe there has to
be a place for all of us, and Cedric found his.

"For a short time after his arrival, he thought he
was in seventh heaven. He found himself among
scientists, but when he began to talk about the laws of
nature they reacted with amazement; for them, there
were no laws as such, but only chances, good or bad.

"Clearly, they understood better than he did such
principles as Heisenberg's, so, though remaining
permanently on guard, he cautiously voiced his own
theory. To all appearances it struck his listeners as
perfectly tenable. He had never met such open-
minded people. They granted him the facilities he

asked for, better than those he had been accustomed to. He drafted a major speech to be delivered at a scientific congress, and in the meantime set about recruiting a group of followers who declared themselves willing to accept his primary axiom: *The universe is out to get us!* With them, he planned to pack the audience at his first public appearance.

"He carried on in this manner for quite some while. His students were fascinated by his arguments, and many let themselves be seduced; reporters came to interview him, and quoted his words fairly. A major foundation consented to fund him after only one appeal for money. Cedric's was at last a famous name.

"Then, when it came time to address the congress, he put on his smartest clothes and shook countless hands and mounted the rostrum. Slides had been prepared; he commentated on them, each in turn, and quoted the notes of all his best experiments.

"Not until he was halfway through the talk did he become aware that some of his hearers had begun to laugh. He carried on, and even reached the end, despite the tides of mirth that now assailed him. One last fragment of hope remained to him, as guffawing was supplanted by applause, and he saw the congress president rise to offer his hand. He still believed, even at that final moment, that he had persuaded his listeners to accept his views.

"But then the congress president said, with absolute sincerity: 'Sir, you have amused us better than any speaker I remember. This notion that the universe is motivated by a kind of planned malevolence has led to so many good jokes one can quote at parties that we're all indebted. When may we look forward to some serious work of equal brilliance?'

"In that moment, Cedric realized he had been right all along. The universe was not only malignant, but capable of outsmarting him, or anyone."

Despite her wet clothes and uncomfortable posture, Anastasia was drowsing at his side. He nudged her gently.

"Don't go to sleep—you mustn't! We have to keep our eyes peeled for the boat."

"Kaloyiannis is so late," she whispered, lids still lowered. "He should have been here long ago."

"We have to go on waiting," he insisted, even as his weariness betrayed him also into slumber.

"Well, now we can arrest him for murder," said Graumann. "And Kaloyiannis as an accessory. I did say—didn't I?—it would be stupid to let the fishing fleet sail tonight, even though the islanders may go hungry without its catch. Know what's amiss with you, *Herr Leutnant*? You don't yet feel the Reich's remorseless logic in your bones."

4

THE EXHIBIT

is a glass preserving jar with a wire closure to its lid.
It commemorates a vanished age of luxury

THE MONTH

is July

THE NAME

is Shanti

T HE STEAM YACHT *MEDEA* WAS SMALL COMPARED TO
some of her kind—nothing like so large, for
example, as those being built in America by Commo-
dore Vanderbilt and others—but she was most luxuri-
ously equipped; the very ensign flying at her stern
was made of silk. Teak, mahogany, gold leaf and
marble abounded in her staterooms, and everywhere
below the main deck there was thick carpet to absorb
the noise of her ultramodern compound engines.

A short while ago, however, those engines had
gradually ceased to turn and there had been a rattling
of anchor chains.

Waiting for the inevitable report from her captain
and engineer, gazing absently at the plume of smoke
which now rose straight up from the *Medea*'s funnel,
her owner Lord Arthur Fenton said languidly, "You
know, Osman old fellow, there are times when I think
it may not have been such a good idea to fall in with

your suggestion of cruising to Constantinople. Not at this time of year, at any rate."

He was a slender, brown-haired man, still under thirty, of middle height, wearing a light linen suit of the most impeccable London cut. He was stretched out on a chaise longue on the afterdeck, in the shade of a canvas awning; it was a blazing July day, and the thermometers were registering ninety. Between him and the person he addressed, who occupied an identical chaise longue, there stood a small table bearing a box of Egyptian cigarettes in paper striped with faint gray lines, a bottle of whisky, a double-globe soda syphon enclosed in wire mesh, and a stock of glasses. His man, who was called Tompkins, sat sweating at a discreet distance, alert for any call to replenish the drinks.

Osman Effendi, who was about the same age, equally well dressed, but somewhat shorter and swarthier, with a thick black mustache on his upper lip and a fez on his head which he somehow contrived to keep in position even when lying down, signaled his own servant Mustapha to hand him another of the cigarettes; he smoked incessantly. While it was being lighted for him, he thought desperately about his response. He had met Lord Arthur in Monte Carlo, and been overjoyed at the chance to make his acquaintance, for he was manifestly very rich, and it would be immensely useful to Osman in the future were he to enjoy wealthy contacts in the world's wealthiest nation. Since it was an unfashionable time of year for the Riviera, with little society to keep one amused, he had indeed proposed this cruise, and sung the praises of his home city until the Englishman

consented. However, things were not going as
smoothly as one might have hoped . . . He decided
at last that it was safest to try and turn the comment
with a joke.

"Ah, perhaps in such heat even your excellent
British engines have decided we Mediterranean types
are correct in taking a siesta!"

"We'll soon know," Lord Arthur grunted. "Here
come Wilson and Macalister."

Snapping to attention as he arrived at his employer's side, the yacht's captain gave a naval-style salute.
Behind him, scowling, her little Scottish engineer
wiped perspiration from his forehead with a grimy
rag.

"Trouble, I'm afraid, m'lord," Wilson said.

"Can it be fixed? If so, how soon?"

"Macalister says it may take five or six hours."

"Really?"—raising one eyebrow. "What's amiss?"

The engineer stepped forward. "The oil we bought
in Italy," he answered curtly. "One of the shaft
bearings has seized. We'll have to unship it and—"

But Lord Arthur was waving explanations aside. He
said, "Just get us on the move again as quick as may
be."

"Yes, of course, m'lord," Wilson agreed.

When they had gone, Lord Arthur rose to his feet
and began to pace distractedly back and forth. "Well,
there's a thing!" he said in exasperation, though his
tone when addressing his underlings had betrayed no
sign of it. "I foresee a boring day, don't you?"

And gestured for Tompkins to mix him another
chota peg.

Hurt, for it was in no way his fault if the oil the
engineer had bought in Italy was of such bad quality,

Osman stared around, screwing up his eyes against the brilliant sun. They had cast anchor off the southern tip of one of the countless islands that littered this part of the world. Spotting it, he had a sudden inspiration.

"It's nearly time for lunch, is it not? Perhaps we could go ashore and make a picnic!"

He greatly prided himself on his knowledge of British culture.

Lord Arthur brightened. "It would pass the time, at least. That is, if there's a decent beach. Tompkins, fetch a telescope!"

It was promptly brought. Surveying the island, he said eventually, "Why, yes. One might well do that. I notice a shack of some sort, though, and there's a woman in front of it staring at us. I trust there won't be too many other folk around. Your people are less than popular in Greece, I understand, and one has no wish to provoke a riot."

Oh, these tactless English! . . . But Osman bridled his tongue. He said only, "In a way, we were as glad to be shut of them as they of us. You should meet some of the thieving, cheating traders that they breed. Anyway, that's history now, isn't it? And I can assure you from long acquaintance that they yield as easily as anyone to the power of money."

Lord Arthur was paying no attention, the telescope still to his eye. "Good lord!" he breathed. "That fellow—Here, take a look for yourself."

Osman adjusted the focus, bracing himself on one of the poles of the awning against the shift and ripple of the water. He saw the woman clearly: young, with quite a good figure—so far as could be judged under her coarse brown ankle-length dress, but she was unlikely to be corseted—and long untidy dark hair. At her side now stood, with one arm protectively around her, a thin man wearing a shabby shirt and a pair of seaman's trousers with one leg torn at the knee. Both were barefoot.

At first Osman did not realize what had so astonished his companion; to him, they looked like any other peasant couple. Then he realized: of course, the man was not just sunburned, but black. Having been accustomed all his life to negro servants and eunuchs, this had not immediately struck him as unusual.

Handing back the telescope, he shrugged.

"The man looks strong and healthy. If we rattle a few coins he will no doubt be glad enough to help carry our things ashore. One should not, however, pay attention to his woman."

"I'm not inclined to," Lord Arthur said fastidiously. "But so long as the place doesn't reek of their sewage . . . Tompkins, tell the stewards to make up a hamper."

"Who are they?" whispered Anastasia. "What do they want with us?"

"I think they stopped because they must. Look, there is no more smoke from the funnel."

Evgenos knew about things like steamships, indeed had traveled on some, but she had only ever seen one before and from a greater distance. Trembling, she watched as a boat was loaded and lowered, and rowed toward the shore.

"I will go down to meet them," Evgenos decided.

"Wait!" She caught his arm. "One of them is

wearing the fez!" The last Turks to lord it over Oragalia had been slaughtered long before she was born, but her foster parents had told her many stories about their cruelty.

"Yes, but that is the flag of the country which helped Greece to become free." Evgenos pointed to the yacht's stern. "We must greet them with pride. Both of us."

"Very well." But she remained near the shack.

The boat grounded in shallow water, still some distance from dry land. In obedience to an order Evgenos did not understand, one of its passengers took off his shoes, rolled up his trousers, and waded ashore. In pidgin Greek he said, "Here is an English lord and his friend. Want to eat food here. You help, you will be paid. Come with me."

Evgenos was dismayed. He said, "But we have nothing to give a lord! We have little enough for ourselves!"

The man was smiling patronizingly. "No, no! We bring own food for them. You help carry, yes? Not take from you nothing. Here, see?"

And he offered a couple of shiny new coins.

Uncertainly Evgenos accepted them—they came to as much as he was paid for a month of casual labor with the fishing fleet—and after biting them tucked them into his cheek, for lack of any other way to carry them. Then he waded to the boat.

"You take lord on shoulders," he was told, and the lord, who luckily was quite light, clambered laughing over the side of the boat and was borne ashore. His friend with the fez was the next, but not the last, burden. Along with the two sailors who had been rowing, and the man who had come ashore first and another servant, Evgenos had now to bring load after load: first, poles and a roll of canvas, which were assembled to make a shady canopy; then folding chairs; then a folding table; then an immense wicker hamper that held, along with dishes and cutlery, something round and bright and brassy that gave off a pale blue flame when a match was set to it, and a seemingly endless supply of food and bottles of wine.

He felt his eyes grow round with amazement, and they all chuckled. Embarrassed, he called to Anastasia.

"Here, these people mean us no harm!"

She descended timidly to join him, and he explained about the English lord. To him, she made a sort of rough curtsy, and he spoke to her kindly enough in what Evgenos guessed was meant to be Greek, though the pronunciation was unfamiliar. But her eyes were full of hatred and suspicion whenever she looked at the man in the fez.

Shortly the visitors were ensconced in luxury, eating and drinking, and Evgenos decided it was time to withdraw. Leading Anastasia back to the shack, he showed her the money he had been given, and she agreed that it was worth his trouble. Then she resumed the task of tending their vegetable patch, while he sat on a rock waiting for his trousers to dry and gazing—not without envy—at the picnickers.

"My Greek didn't make much impression, did it?" said Lord Arthur. "Your man Mustapha did better! Any more champagne in that bottle?"

Tompkins darted to refill his glass.

"Of course," he went on, "one wouldn't expect to find the language of Plato and Sophocles in a corner like this. It looks as barren as the worst part of the Highlands, only without so much water. What do you suppose these people do to survive? One can't exactly call it living, can one?"

Osman shrugged; he cared little about such matters. "I imagine they rely on fishing," he said after a pause, and signaled Mustapha to light him another cigarette.

"The way that blackamoor is staring at us," Lord Arthur murmured, "one would think he had us in mind for his next catch . . . Finished?"

"What? Oh—oh, yes. And thank you very much: the potted pheasant was particularly good."

"I'm glad you liked it. Shot it myself at Ardnacraish last year. I must admit I was wondering whether it would have stood the heat, but our cook up there is a positive marvel . . . Are you sure you won't have an orange? No? How about a drop of brandy?"

"Yes, with pleasure!"

"Tompkins!"

For a while there was a pleasantly sated pause. Eventually, however, Lord Arthur started to fidget.

"He's still staring at us, you know. And if those great eyes of his were proboscises, he'd have sucked us in!"

"My dear fellow, I assure you there's nothing to worry about! He wouldn't dare try anything. He's outnumbered, to begin with, and your engineer assured us we shall be away before nightfall. Besides, there's another point to consider. You said my kind were unpopular here; well, his are even more so, and indeed I'm astonished that he's found himself a woman. Conceivably she—ah—disgraced herself and was driven out by her family, and he was the only man around to take her on. They're not as choosy as civilized people, you know."

"How do you suppose he came to be here in the first place?"

"Arthur, sometimes you puzzle me. What in the world do you find interesting about nonentities like these?"

Lord Arthur stretched and yawned. "Anything can seem interesting when there's nothing else to provide a distraction. And—to quote you—there's another point to consider."

"Such as, for instance?"

"Well, with all due respect, your empire is in decline and ours on the ascendant. Could it not have something to do with the fact that your beys and pashas and so forth take too little interest in the lives of the people they rule over? If you compare our record in India with yours in, say, Rumelia—"

Lord Arthur was drunk again. In a large company he was often entertainingly so; during the cruise, however, Osman had learned that he could be offensive, albeit in the nicest possible way, when there were only the two of them. Hastily he said, "You could always call them down and ask them. Myself, I suspect he's only staring at us because he never had a square meal in his life, and he's wondering what will become of the scraps we've left."

"You're right! Dammit, you must be right! Well, when in Rome! . . ." Lord Arthur jumped to his feet, waving. In execrably pronounced—though grammatical—ancient Greek he called to the black man and his woman, who, tired from her labor, was now sitting at his side. They gazed back blankly until Mustapha came to the rescue.

"Lord want give you food too!"

At that they approached, hand in hand, but not hurrying. Watching them, Osman plucked the Englishman's sleeve.

"They are probably unaccustomed, you know, to chairs and tables!"

"Hmm! That's a point!" Lord Arthur looked around, and spotted an oblong plank of wood which the chance of the waves had lodged in a crevice along the rocky shore. He pointed at it.

"They might be more comfortable if they ate off that, you mean? Very well! Tompkins, fetch it, will you?"

His servant hastened to obey, but turned the board over and over as he returned, staring at it with curiosity.

"What's the matter, man?" Lord Arthur demanded.

"There's some sort of painting on it, sir," Tompkins answered, and held up one side for inspection.

Lord Arthur glanced at it, and Osman said anxiously, "Why! It's a religious image, isn't it?" He spoke with all the distaste of a good Moslem, forbidden to make images for purposes of worship.

"Ah, yes!" Lord Arthur screwed a monocle into his right eye and examined the weather-worn traces of paint the wood still bore. "Looks like a crude depiction of a Virgin and Child. Fascinating, this primitive art, don't you think? But I take your point. They might be offended if we made them use it as a table, mightn't they? Oh, well! I suppose they're used to eating off the bare ground . . . It's too late, anyway. Here they come. That's what they'll have to put up with."

With a certain dignity the black man bowed, accepted an invitation to sit down in the shade—though the woman knelt, and for the first time they noticed that she was pregnant—and when given the leftover food made sure that she had the choicest portions.

"Hmm! Not so savage," Lord Arthur approved. "Don't think much of their table manners, but then my own ancestors ate with their fingers, I believe, until forks were introduced from Italy. Tompkins, don't broach any more of that champagne, but I imagine we could spare a bottle of claret if the Turkish wines are as good as Osman Effendi claims. Come to that, I wouldn't mind a drop!"

And, gravely, the guests both drank to his health.

"Talk about noble savages!" Lord Arthur exclaimed. "I wonder whether that's natural, inborn, inshtinctive, or—" And checked, as he realized that a tricky word had just tripped him up. Leaning back, he turned to Mustapha, who understood a little English and French as well as Greek and Turkish.

"You! Ask him what he's called and how he came here!"

At first Evgenos answered reluctantly; then the wine loosened his tongue, and he admitted he had been born in slavery and never known his parents. A little boastfully, he made it clear that he had not been freed, but run away, although, with many nervous glances at Osman, he declined to mention who had been his owner.

"Good for you, then!" cried Lord Arthur recklessly, and waved for Tompkins to refill their glasses. "We abolished slaves in England! Land of the free and all that, you know!"

After skimming off all possible profit from the trade, Osman glossed silently. With his host in this mood, he did not dare voice the thought.

Sometimes, though, he did wonder whether he had chosen the right course by westernizing himself. The arguments he always had to endure when he called on his father . . . But here was someone else, albeit very humble, who seemed to have had no qualms about making an analogous decision. Wine had lent his woman Anastasia courage, too, and when Evgenos hesitated over explaining their relationship she spoke up for the first time.

"I am an orphan. This is a little island. There are few men. All are my cousins. Trade is not good. The spirit has gone out of the families that own the land. My uncle who adopted me thought most about joining another estate to his. I did not want the husband he decided on. Too many women marry their cousins because there is nobody else. I don't mind Evgenos being a stranger. He is strong and everybody knows how hard he can work. One day they'll accept him because already we are growing good food on land the others left. My uncle may die angry but I still like his daughter. Her husband treats her badly and now she is jealous of my good luck, but she will get over that. Even my aunts say now that I may have been right after all."

Singling out one comment from the approximate version Mustapha was able to provide, Lord Arthur burst into loud laughter.

"Your cousin is jealous of your good luck, is she? How amazing! Well, one won't ask what kind of luck! Eh, Osman?"—this with a nudge in his companion's ribs.

The latter remained silent, not so much because he was growing sleepy from the heat and the wine and brandy as because he had been raised never to speak of what transpired in the *harēmlik*, the "lawful" part of the house.

At just that moment, however, there was a hoot from the yacht's steam siren, and they all glanced toward her. A plume of gray was rising from her funnel again, and on her foredeck a sailor was signaling with colored flags.

"Well, good for Macalister!" exclaimed Lord Arthur. "I should know him well enough by this time to realize that when he means one hour he'll say two, to be on the safe side. Bloody pessimist! Let's clear up and get aboard."

"Excuse me, m'lord," Tompkins ventured, "but how much of this food do you want taken back? The potted meats won't last now they've been opened, and some of the fruit—"

"Oh!"—with a grand gesture. "The nigger can have it! And a bottle of wine too, provided he carries me back to the boat without getting my feet wet."

When the steam yacht had departed, trailing her smoke into the sunset like a vast flag, Evgenos helped Anastasia to gather up the remnants and carry them to their shack.

"I told you they wouldn't harm us," he chided, his

mouth full of English ham and pickles and stale but white bread.

"Yet they were afraid we might harm them," she muttered, propping against the center post of their shack what she had reclaimed as a particular treasure, the icon of the Virgin and Child which the sea had tossed ashore.

"Why should we? How could they think such a thing?"

"Because they are so insecure in their luxury."

"But here, left for us as presents, are delicacies such as I have never tasted! The glass jars these pickles came in, just to start with, are finer than—"

She waved him to silence, seizing the wine bottle and drinking deeply.

"Their confidence is an illusion. All of it depends on how efficiently we can be cowed, like me at sight of that red fez. I'm ashamed. It makes me think of Shanti."

Replete, content, he lay back in the warm evening air and listened to her tale as darkness fell.

"Now Shanti was a soft and undemanding person, chosen for reasons contrary to those affecting Cedric. Her, and her parents', culture encouraged her to be passive. She expected the world to treat her well, but when it didn't, though she certainly knew how to complain, she had no faintest notion how to act. She did, however, have hopes, and ultimately they were—in a sense—fulfilled.

"The place she came to was exactly what she'd always dreamed of. It was a benign and hospitable world, where no one had to work. The climate was delightful and the people could go without clothes, though there were many kinds of ornament and decoration. When you felt hungry, there was no need to do more than look for fallen fruit and nuts, or the shellfish which abounded at the seaside. Also there were animals so tame they seemed almost to welcome an invitation to be slaughtered, but they were killed only with great ceremony and on certain feast days that everyone looked forward to for months beforehand, when a sweet intoxicating drink was served and all made merry. Even a storm provided entertainment, in the form of lightning. Much of the people's music imitated thunder, too, for if a cloudburst washed away a house or two, then felling a few trees and weaving leaves to make new roofs and walls likewise offered a distraction and an excuse for a party. Besides, rainwater filled the drinking ponds.

"Also there were other kinds of pleasure. She proved attractive to a lot of men, with the entire approval of their wives. Some of the latter too decided to test what their husbands had reported on so well, and pronounced themselves equally satisfied. In a short while she was famous, insofar as fame existed in that place, and a great feast was mounted in her honor."

Anastasia paused to reach for the wine again, and he urged her, "Tell the rest!"

"There wasn't any 'rest,'" she said. "That was the beginning and the end, endlessly repeated."

5

THE EXHIBIT

is a warped board painted blue, silver, gold and red.
It serves to summarize a faith rejected

THE MONTH

is August

THE NAME

is Giacomo

DURING THE HOT AUGUST NIGHT ANASTASIA HAD tossed aside the thin rough sheet she shared with Evgenos. Just at dawn there came the faintest, faintest wisp of breeze, and the change in temperature awakened her. Stretching languorously, out of habit she reached to reclaim their cover, but checked in mid-movement, sniffing the air.

"Evgenos!" she exclaimed suddenly. "Quick!"

And jumped up, seizing her tattered dress.

He roused more slowly, but as soon as he came to himself he perceived what had excited her. Faint, yet unmistakable, a most delectable smell had drifted into the hovel they called home, as though the beach, the island, the very sea had been planted with richly perfumed flowers. With a mutter of amazement he drew on his breeches.

"What do you think it can be?" he demanded.

She said something wild about a vision of saints and angels. Only in heaven could there be such fragrance!

More cynical, yet confused enough to imagine she might be right, he thrust aside the tatters that hung across the doorway and emerged blinking in new daylight.

No saints. No angels. Nothing miraculous. But something remarkable, nonetheless. Just offshore lay one of the greatest ships that plied these waters: a Venetian galley laden above deck and below with the most aromatic spices the Orient could offer—nutmegs, cinnamon, pepper, cassia, cloves . . . How many tons in all she carried, he could not guess, but it was enough to scent the air for miles around.

At first there was no sign of activity on board. This breeze, this zephyr, was not even strong enough to stir the burgee flying from her mainmast, let alone fill the canvas brailed below its crosstree. Her kedge was down and her oars were shipped, indicating that her rowers were exhausted. The notion crossed Evgenos's mind that she might have been struck by plague, in which case she was a terrifying apparition. Then again, of course, if her crew were suffering nothing worse than weariness and thirst, and if he swam out to her with skin bottles of good sweet water from the spring beyond the headland . . .

Dreams of rescue and reward were dashed a moment later. Three figures appeared on deck, rubbing sleep from their eyes, and shortly caught sight of him and Anastasia. They waved. She waved back frantically. There was the sound of shouted orders, and the ship came slowly back to life.

In a while, a dinghy was lowered, and three people—possibly the same three, though the distance was too great for Evgenos to be certain—set out for shore, two rowing and the third in the stern, using another oar for a rudder.

"How wonderful!" Anastasia breathed. "They must be very rich! Perhaps we can sell them something for a lot of money!"

More cynically Evgenos said, "Most rich people get rich by taking what they want without paying for it. It's the way of the world."

He wished he possessed a weapon that would symbolize his determination to defend against all comers himself, the woman he was so proud of having won, and this patch of ungrateful land that yielded them their meager living. For a moment he thought of the sword he had found as he strove to dig it . . . but though its hilt and guard were intact its blade was a rusty stub. What else might serve him if the need arose?

Glancing around, he caught sight of the wooden pole, sharpened at one end, which they used to furrow the patch of dusty, salty ground between their home and the beach. Apart from his fisherman's gutting knife, it was as good a weapon as they owned. Taking hold of it, he tried to lean on it with a casual air, as though it were nothing more than a stick to relieve strain on a gammy leg.

Anastasia wanted to rush down to the water's edge and greet the strangers. He checked her with a touch.

"Wait until we see how they behave. Wait until we hear what they've got to say."

"But they're foreign! You can't understand foreigners!"

"I've been to places you had never even heard of,

you know that. I picked up a little of the *lingua franca* and I think I may remember just enough."

Compliant, she obeyed.

The dinghy grounded in the shallows. One of the rowers jumped out: a thin boy wearing salt-crusted breeches and a shirt with one sleeve ripped away. He produced a splintered plank and laid it from the bow to a rock that offered dry footing. Stowing his steering oar, the man from the stern picked his way forward and, balancing nimbly, walked the plank to land. It would be fair to guess he was the captain of the galley. He too was thin, of medium height, with a hawk-beaked nose above a dense black beard. A brown velvet slouch cap shaded his piercing eyes. Like the rest of his clothing—a gray shirt that had been white, a plum-colored velvet doublet with its pile rubbed away on the right side, black breeches tucked into wide boots with their tops turned over—it had no doubt once been fine and costly, but now his whole attire was stained and shabby.

Evgenos kept his face mask-stiff, striving to look like a stupid peasant. But he was plagued by a terrible sense of disorientation, as though from drinking too much wine. Every time he looked closely at the newcomers, he seemed to see more than one of them, blurred and out of focus.

Then the stranger did something that took him totally aback. He broke into a broad grin and advanced with arm outstretched.

"Gene! Stacy!" he exclaimed. "How are you?"

Bewildered, they drew back, and Anastasia caught at Evgenos's free hand, squeezing his fingers so hard it almost hurt.

For no one, short of eavesdropping on their pallet stuffed with moss and prickly fern, could have known about the pet names they called each other! Evgenos tightened his grip on the sharpened pole, uncertain whether it would be wise to show defiance, yet ashamed not to.

At all events, this stranger spoke a language he could understand after a fashion. Framing words with difficulty, because most of the time he and Anastasia had little to talk about—there was no news on Oragalia, only scandal and rumor—he said, "Who are you? What do you want?"

It was the captain's turn to be taken aback. Lowering his hand, he said uncertainly, "But—Oh, surely, you must remember me? Stacy!"

Wide-eyed, Anastasia shook her head. A lock of her lank and greasy hair fell over one eye; hastily she brushed it back. She should not have been out here, in the presence of strange men, wearing just a dress and with nothing to cover her head. But she was too frightened now to risk going in search of a shawl.

"Look!" His expression affable enough, but his voice full of puzzlement, the captain approached more closely. "You must recognize me, surely! I'm *****!"

However, if what followed was a name, then it was one they couldn't repeat—couldn't even register. It was full of wrong sounds, such as they had never attempted to twist their tongues around. It was as much like hearing double as looking at the visitors resembled seeing double . . . yet neither was a right comparison. Evgenos fought against the sickening sensation with all his might.

"What do you want?" he demanded again. "Is it water for your crew? We can give you drink if you leave us in peace, but we have nothing fine enough to be worth stealing!"

The captain stood irresolute for a moment, glancing at his companions; by now they had moored the dinghy and joined him. The second rower was large and burly, with a scarred face and a dirty kerchief tied around his right forearm, patched with brown as from dried blood.

"What do you make of this, #####?" the captain demanded. Once again the name defeated Evgenos's ear. As the boy the question was addressed to shook his head, he decided to think of him as Bony, and the burly one as Scarface.

"You, ‡‡‡‡‡?" This time the captain appealed to the latter.

"We'll have to ask a lot more questions," Scarface rumbled.

"I don't like these people!" Anastasia whispered. "Do something to make them go away!"

Equally softly, Evgenos returned, "A far cry from saints and angels, aren't they? But how can I drive them off? All I can do is persuade them there's nothing here to interest them . . ." And he added more loudly, "Didn't you hear me say we're not worth robbing?"

"We don't even have enough food for ourselves!" Anastasia chimed in loudly. "We don't know how we'll manage when the baby comes!" And she laid her hand dramatically on the rising curve of her belly.

"Ah, yes! That's one of the things I've come to see you about." The captain adopted a soothing tone.

"Don't you think it would be better for your baby to be born in a /hospital/, in /sterile/ conditions with trained staff on hand, rather than in your cave? What about /amniocentesis/? What about your /rhesus incompatibility/? You were told you're /rhesus opposites/; you can't have forgotten that! Of course, you'll be a /primapara/, so your system hasn't been sensitized, but even so you're running a terrible risk, let alone the danger of /Down's syndrome/ if you have your first child at such an advanced age . . . Oh, hell! It's no use, is it? I'm not getting through."

He turned away despondently. After a pause Bony suggested, "What about something on a more basic level? They seem to be afraid that we're here to rob them, don't they? But we can easily disabuse them of that idea."

"Yes, of course!" Scarface agreed. "We can bring a load of provisions, the sort of stuff they can't have seen in months, and gain their attention that way. How about it?"

Bewildered, Evgenos and Anastasia looked from one to the other of the intruders, striving to make sense of what was being said, and failing.

"It's worth trying," the captain agreed. "Go ahead!"

At once Bony and Scarface relaunched the dinghy and made haste toward the galley, whose crew were now fully awake and going about their normal business of checking the rigging and washing down the decks.

"Gene! Stacy! Shall we sit down?" the captain proposed, and suited action to word by lowering his rump gingerly on to a flattish rock.

"How does he know our private names?" Anastasia whispered, making no move to copy him.

"I don't know," Evgenos answered grimly, still fighting the impulse to see and hear two, or twenty, where there was only one. "Saints and angels, hmm? I could better believe them devils! Fetch the icon!"

They had one hanging over their pallet, the only gift at their wedding—about which most of the islanders had been furious—that might last a while beyond the birth of their first child; the rest of the presents had been scraps of cloth, pickled vegetables and salted fish, jars of oil and the like, the smallest tokens the givers thought they could get away with. It was painted in cheap colors on a slab of badly warped wood, but it had been properly dedicated in the church and carried the power of the image on it, the Virgin and Child in blue, red, white and gold.

Thanks to Anastasia's habit of kissing it night and morning, though, much of the paint in the center had already worn away.

She made haste to unhook the string on which it hung from the natural peg afforded by a branch stump on the tree trunk Evgenos had set up as the hovel's center post (and there had been a row about its felling, for some declared it had stood beyond the border of the unclaimed ground where they had made their home—but it had yielded nothing, it wasn't an olive and it didn't bear nuts, so it was no great loss).

Rushing back, she held the icon before her like a shield, affected by Evgenos's mention of devils to the point where it seemed she expected the captain to scream and disappear.

But the latter's only reaction was to take it from her for inspection. "I take it you're very proud of this," he remarked, smiling as he handed it back. "So you should be. It must be very old. I'm no expert, of course, but to me it looks like a splendid example of traditional folk art. It could well fetch thousands at an auction in @@@@@."

Where?

Once again a name slithered past their ears. Baffled, on the verge of crying, Anastasia clutched the icon to her breast and hurried to restore it to its usual place.

By this time, however, Evgenos had accepted that they were in no immediate danger. Laying by his intended means of defense, he cautiously sat down on another level rock, facing the captain. He said, "How is it you seem to know us? I don't recognize you at all."

He made no mention of the countless others he could see whenever he looked at him.

"Are you sure? Don't you think it might come back to you in a little while?"

"But where did we meet? I don't remember!"

Gravely, the captain leaned forward, elbow on knee and chin in hand.

"That's fairly obvious," he said with a frown. "The question remains: why not? How what you've been through could have affected you so deeply on the mental level, even though physically both you and Stacy seemed perfectly normal on your return: *that's* what we don't understand."

"Return from where?" Evgenos cried. "Where did I go?"

"If I could tell you that," said the captain soberly, "we wouldn't be talking in riddles, would we? But you and Stacy have been there, and I haven't. Don't you realize how much we admire you both? You must be among the bravest people in history. Knowing how poor your chances were, you went ahead and volunteered because you cared more about your species than yourselves. If only—"

Evgenos sat dumb, letting the incomprehensible words flow on. He had never done anything more admirable than run away to this island in search of sanctuary. His memory assured him that was the truth.

Though, of course, meeting and winning Anastasia . . .

But these people hadn't come here after women, or anything else. In fact, they seemed to be bringing rather than taking away. In the distance the dinghy had been loaded with a cargo he could not clearly discern, and Bony and Scarface were bending to their oars again. Meantime, as Anastasia hastened back and dropped on her knees at his side, as though into protective shelter, he forced out, "You didn't finish what you were saying."

"Oh, yes. I was about to say: if only there were some way we could get reports without sending live observers! Or if only we could devise some sort of training program to prepare people for what they're going to encounter! But we simply can't conceive /machines/ that will react along the same lines. Our brains don't work the way /computers/ do. You know, for years we've had a prize on offer, worth ten million plus the assurance of worldwide fame, for anyone who can design a /machine/ capable of passing the /interface/ and returning with decipherable data. Frankly, I don't think anyone is going to win it who hasn't

John Brunner

already made the trip—Ah! I see breakfast coming. I hope you're hungry."

When had either of them been otherwise?

But Evgenos held his tongue, and allowed himself to be persuaded into helping to unload the dinghy. Its cargo proved to consist of foodstuffs as strange and fascinating as the scent he and Anastasia had awoken to.

Friendly and generous, the captain passed squat goblets of a substance that was warmer to the touch than glass or pottery, tinted throughout with bright intrinsic colors and every one different. These were then filled by Bony with a steaming dark brown liquid which, when sipped, made them alert and lively. Bread followed; though cool, it was as moist and spongy as if it had come fresh from the oven. To go with it there were pinkish brown cylinders of chopped meat, spicy and delicious, preserves sweeter than any Evgenos could remember tasting, strange bright red fruit with yellow pips, and more, and more, and more . . .

"This is a /tomato/," the captain explained. "What you are drinking is /coffee/ and—well, you obviously recognize bread, but those are /frankfurters/ and the pickle is /mango chutney/ and this is a /bell pepper/ and this is . . ."

No use. The blank wall remained between them. Evgenos was aware that he and Anastasia were expected to respond in some way to these unfamiliar, though welcome, foods, whose names he heard and instantly forgot, but when he strove to think of any connection they might have with his past, he failed. Glancing at Anastasia, he saw that she was equally at a

91

loss, though she ate greedily. Contrariwise Scarface, Bony, and the captain, all three, displayed small appetite, concerned only to produce more and more of what they had brought in the hope of—what? What could they be looking for on Oragalia, this island forgotten by the rest of the world? They couldn't be hoping to open up a new market for their exotic imports! Who on this poverty-stricken hummock of rock and sand could afford to pay their prices?

Replete, burping, Evgenos waved aside the latest offering. Never had he dreamed of such a banquet, least of all one conjured up without warning on his own patch of salt-sour ground! The finest feasts held at the island's single village, where people vied with one another to have their neighbors admire their skill in drying fish, preparing oil and wine, or pickling onions, paled into insignificance beside this repast . . . whose hosts apparently regarded it as trivial, judging by the way they were tossing the leftovers into the sea. For a second he was angered: why, he and Anastasia could have made two more meals off what was being wasted!

Then he recovered himself. He owed the visitors something, in the way of courtesy if no other. He turned to the captain, relieved at seeing only one of him by now.

"Sir, will you not tell me when and where you think I met you?"

"Not just you," the other answered. "Stacy as well."

"That's impossible!" Anastasia burst out. "I've spent my whole life on this island! The only people I've ever met were born here, same as me, or came like you across the sea. And I never saw a ship like yours before, and most of all I never saw *you*! Unless—"

A horrifying idea struck her. She rounded on Evgenos.

"Unless you had another woman before you came here who was so like me that this man has mixed us up!"

"Now you're being silly!" the captain began, rising to his feet. But Anastasia did the same, more swiftly.

"I don't know you!" she cried. "I don't want to know you or the world you come from! I didn't invite you here and all I want is for you to go away!"

Bursting into tears, she spun on her heel and fled to the shelter of the cave above their hovel.

Instantly angry on her behalf, Evgenos lifted his pole, prepared to strike the captain down, but Scarface laid a hand on his arm and warned him to desist. Bony said, "We're wasting our time, you know. It's just as I've been predicting all along: this sort of direct approach can only drive them deeper into /fugue/."

"But we can't just leave them to rot!" the captain exclaimed. "Especially now she's pregnant!"

"There's time yet," Bony countered. "And if nothing breaks before her waters—sorry: bad joke—we'll simply have to intervene on the grandest possible scale. Meantime there's no special hurry."

"No hurry? Are you crazy?" The captain took half a pace back.

"There are some cases," Scarface said grayly, "where haste is self-defeating. We literally do not know what's going on. It could even be that this is the penalty the cosmos imposes on creatures as hubristic as ourselves."

"Stuff your /mystical/ nonsense!" the captain flared.

"When we're dealing not just with the frontiers of reality, but something way beyond them, there isn't a divide between /science/ and /mysticism/ anymore." With a smile of apology Scarface let go Evgenos's arm.

"Well said," approved the boy he had privately nicknamed Bony, and turned away. "So long, Gene. Apologize to Stacy on our behalf. We didn't mean to make her so upset."

Evgenos was on the verge of demanding that they stay and explain themselves properly, when in sudden amazement he thought: *boy?* And realized Bony wasn't one, but a woman, for all her masculine disguise.

Confused beyond measure, he was glad to see them go.

As always, a couple of hours after noon, the heat of the land began to draw cooler air off the sea. That, plus the beating of the water by the galley's oars, dispersed the dense and aromatic vapor from her cargo. When it had faded completely, Anastasia and Evgenos were left with a vague feeling of regret, or unfulfillment.

But at least they had a respite from hunger. The scraps the visitors had left would suffice them for days, even though some had had to be retrieved from the shallows and were soaked with salt water.

"Those people . . ." Gene muttered as darkness fell.

"Yes?"

"Wasn't it strange how they thought we used to know them?"

"Hah!" she retorted caustically. "Some people are

vain enough to believe they ought to be recognized anywhere!"

He gave a dry chuckle. "Yes, that's part of it, I guess. And yet . . ."

"What?" Undressing amid yawns, ready to stretch out on their crude bed, she added, "Aren't you tired?"

"Yes—yes, very tired." Not rising, he started to peel off his shirt, but with it still spread across his knees he spoke again.

"Nonetheless that can't be the whole story. It's obvious enough that people can be lured to make long voyages by the hope of profit, and who would not prize a cargo of spices like the one that scented our whole island today?"

"It could have bought and sold our land a hundred times over!" she exclaimed as she lay down.

"Yes, even perhaps a thousand times." But such enormous numbers felt foreign to them both. He plowed ahead.

"What, though, is one to make of people who travel for the sake of traveling—of finding themselves to-morrow, or next year, in a land no one they ever met or even heard of has set foot upon before? People who are prepared to take the risk of being cast away because they are so greedy for places where every-thing is different from at home!"

"I suppose they're out of their minds," Stacy replied around another yawn.

"No! No!" Warming to his theme, Gene twisted his calloused hands back and forth, back and forth, on the coarse and tattered fabric of his shirt. "Was Giacomo crazy, for example?"

"Maybe."

"Are you? Am I?"

"Maybe."

"But I don't *feel* crazy!"

"What does being crazy feel like? My guess is that it must feel normal."

He considered that awhile, wondering why a woman should dress up as a boy. Eventually he said, "If not, I suppose one could recognize it . . . But that still doesn't take care of people like Giacomo."

"Tell me why not."

"Because he was chronically discontented. He maintained that the only kind of world to suit his restless spirit was one where nothing was ever the same from one day to the next. He declared himself heartily sick of those who, like his father, strove in cobwebbed libraries and gray museums to reduce the cosmos to entries in a catalogue. He dreamed of a universe where there would always be new challenges, new realms to be explored; where people like himself could forever be setting out on journeys into the unknown, and be the bane of those who stayed at home in a boring, dull, predictable environment, occupying themselves with study and analysis. He used to say, 'So you've dissected lots of frogs! Did you ever wind up knowing how to build a frog that did frog things, or were there just more piles of rotten meat to throw away?'

"For him, therefore, the journey was his life's ambition. He set out joyfully and found his goal. In the place he came to, it was axiomatic that tomorrow should be different from today. On learning that he was an explorer by profession, the people eagerly financed his team. So off he went, with comrades of like mind, and found a jungle no one had traversed, replete with the most amazing novelties: relics and tribes, and animals, that none had seen before! He endured privations worse than any he'd imagined; sometimes starving, sometimes half-dead of thirst, losing his companions one by one, he achieved the most epic exploration of all time, and when he staggered back to the coast, leech-weakened, staring-eyed, nearly naked, but clutching to him precious records he'd compiled, he was at long last glad of a chance to return to the city he'd set out from, which lately he'd condemned as dull and smug. He'd been away a year or two at most, so he looked forward to a splendid welcome.

"Yet even at the docks he felt betrayed. The city was certainly the one he had booked passage to, only . . . Here were old, known names, but the signs indicated unfamiliar streets; there were different instructions in the phone booth from which he tried to call a number that turned out not to exist. The cars and trucks were wrongly shaped and made an alien noise, and he did not recognize the coding of their registration plates; the meal he ordered in a café stemmed from a cuisine he did not know, and when he tried to pay for it the money in his pocket was dismissed as a crude forgery. Worst of all, the policemen called by the proprietor arrived in uniforms the like of which he'd never seen before. Only when he was dragged away to jail did he realize the truth."

"I don't understand," Stacy murmured out of shadow.

"Why, that on this world which matched his heart's

desire nothing was stable, nothing remained the same. Had he only stayed where he found himself at first, he could have enjoyed all the benefits of change without the shock of coming home to a city where he and his mission were doomed to be forgotten . . . or derided."

For a while there was silence. Then:

"I still don't see what you mean, but it was a pretty tale anyhow. Before tomorrow, please, let us forget the strangers." Rolling over, Stacy spread wide her arms.

"With the best will in the world," said Gene as he embraced her. "Only—"

"Only what?"

"I think maybe they won't so easily forget us."

"What do you mean?" she exclaimed in alarm, for she had felt him shiver.

A cold and distant fear had touched him. With an effort he dismissed it, and shortly persuaded her that, tonight at least, there was no more need for speech.

6

THE EXHIBIT

is the hilt of a rusty sword, its blade a stub.
It marks the failure of an age of certainty

THE MONTH

is September

THE NAME

is Hedwig

EXCEPT FOR THE VERY YOUNG, THE SICK, AND THE very old, and those who were obliged to stay at home and tend them, the entire population of Oragalia had assembled in the island's single church to mark the festival of the Exaltation of the Holy Cross. They included some whose presence was resented, but the *papas* had ordered slandermongers to bridle their tongues, since it was unbefitting to speak evil of one's fellows at this sacred time.

The drab interior of the building had been transformed, so far as resources allowed, with limewash and bunches of late summer flowers. Bees attracted by the latter buzzed somnolently around, trying to retrace the way they had come in, sometimes evoking cries from children old enough to know they stung, too young to understand that they were a precious gift from the Pantocrator not only for their honey but as a symbol of pain hidden by the sweetness of sin.

In general the spirits of the people were light, for it had been a good summer. There had been no sickness among either the folk or their livestock, the figs and olives were yielding bountifully, and the wild thyme on the hillsides was so fragrant it could be smelled far out to sea. Ill-clad, sunken-eyed, most of the married ones—and the young widows—hollow-cheeked from early loss of teeth, they nonetheless raised their voices loudly and cheerfully, especially in response to the special invocations the *papas* recited for the safety and success of those bound on the latest mission to liberate the Holy Land from domination by the Saracens. The future of the Kingdom of Jerusalem was precarious, or so rumor said, but Christian knights were gathering from all over Europe to its aid, and when they had vanquished the enemy the riches of the Orient would once more come pouring through this quarter of the Middle Sea. A fraction of that fabled wealth must surely wash up on the shore of even so petty an island as Oragalia. Fervently they prayed it would.

And then the outer world broke in on them, sooner than and differently from what they besought the Lord to grant.

Just as the priest was bringing the service to its end, the low main door of the church, closed against the sun's harsh glare, was forced wide with a grating noise; it had dropped on its hinges and it scraped the flagstones. Every eye turned to see who had so belatedly come to answer the call to worship.

Five strangers. Armed strangers. Armed and arrogant.

All their faces were heavily scarred, by battle or

disease or both, and one of them was blind on his right side; all had battered metal helmets on their heads; all carried shields and drawn swords; all wore coats of chain mail, which marked them out as knights, and the first to enter had greaves and gauntlets too; all bar one had carved wooden crosses hanging around their necks on leather thongs; and the exception, the one-eyed man, who hung back in the doorway as his comrades advanced toward the altar, had a sort of amice over his mail, white but badly soiled, with red crosses embroidered on it front and back.

Their leader, the one in almost full armor, stared suspiciously around the little church. Then, relaxing, he sheathed his blade—with a signal that his companions should do the same—and swaggered up to the priest. The congregation shrank against the walls, the women and children seeking shelter at the backs of their menfolk. In the sudden hush could be heard shouts and banging noises from the waterfront. Many fretted for the safety of their prized possessions such as livestock, boats, barrels and fishing nets, but dared not brave the intruders' swords to run and see what was happening.

The knight confronting the *papas* now addressed him in Latin, speaking loudly and slowly as to an idiot. He made himself understood only with difficulty; the priest was a local man, scarcely more than a youth, whose command even of the Greek Testament was less than perfect. But eventually he sighed and turned to his congregation.

"This is the Sieur de Belmaison, a great gentleman from France," he announced. "He has come with a

company of soldiers in two ships. They are bound to
fight the Saracens. They were driven off course by
contrary winds. They are short of food and drink. We
must show them charity because theirs is a sacred
mission. Even if they hold a wrong opinion concerning the Trinity, they too are Christians and all
Christians must band together against the agents of
the Evil One."

Standing beside him with a suspicious expression,
the French lord surveyed the congregation. His gaze
lighted on one particular young woman, and lingered.
Even though she was conspicuously with child, she
had a handsome face and good clear skin. Moreover,
she kept apart from the rest of the people, as though
they made her feel unwelcome. The rest, that was,
except one . . . and he was a strange fellow to find
hereabouts! How far was he from home? What could
possibly have brought to Oragalia a blackamoor
darker than the Saracens themselves?

Instantly de Belmaison jumped to the conclusion
that this outsider must be at least a spy, and possibly
an agent of Satan who had come hither in the hope of
subverting the faith of these simple peasant folk,
undermined as it already was by the falsehoods of the
Eastern Church. The priest had finished interpreting
what he had said so far, and from what snatches he
had been able to understand seemed to have made an
honest job of it. Now he spoke up again, not only
emphasizing the islanders' obligation to show charity
toward their cobelievers, but also warning them
against Mussulmen, pagans, and other evildoers.

This time, when the translation was concluded,

there was a remarkable reaction among the islanders. Everywhere he saw grim nods of agreement, and many harsh glances were cast at the black man and the woman by his side. So, although it was heretical, their religion must be strong enough to resist the fellow's wheedling and cajoling. Excellent. His ship's chaplain would be bound to take a great interest in the matter, though.

"Well, you can guess what we want," he resumed. "It's long and long since we enjoyed bread softer than the rocks of your seashore, or fresh meat, or wine any sweeter than vinegar! Get to it! Do your Christian duty! Or"—and he narrowed his eyes and let his hand stray toward his swordhilt—"we shall feel entitled to help ourselves!"

That provoked a ripple of dismay among the worshipers. Someone said in a whisper meant to be overheard, "What's the betting they already did?"

But de Belmaison failed to understand the coarsely accented Greek, and the *papas* felt no inclination to translate it.

The islanders made haste to disperse. Shortly, however, there were squeals from outside, followed by cries of anger. By the sound of it, someone had found a pig and promptly slaughtered it. A moment later, and a goose and several chickens went the same way. Intending to hang back as usual until everyone else had left, dreadfully conscious of de Belmaison's interest in her and her man, Anastasia whispered to Evgenos, "Will they seize what we have, too?"

They were poor, but they did have a dozen hens, and preserves in store against the winter.

"Not if I can help it!" Evgenos promised. "Let's make for home as quickly as we can!"

And, unprecedentedly, caught her hand and pushed the remaining worshipers aside on their way to the door.

Standing beside it, the one-eyed stranger was inspecting those who passed by, his gaze as keen as anyone's with normal sight. The sunken pit above his right cheekbone lent him a sinister and terrifying air; parents were making their children avert their faces. Anastasia too shrank back and tried to hide behind Evgenos. But, to her and their astonishment, his face softened into half a smile when they arrived before him—half, because whatever wound had cost him his eye had also shriveled the muscles at that corner of his mouth.

In ill-pronounced but comprehensible Greek, he said, "A blessing on your child, young friends. I'm sure he will be tall and strong and handsome."

Anastasia suppressed a shriek of horror and fled into the sunlight, dragging Evgenos after her. Despite their detestation of the black foreigner who had won the favors of the island's prettiest girl, the rest of those in earshot crossed themselves or made the sign of the horns and rushed in Anastasia's wake, leaving the church—apart from the presence of the *papas*—in the undisputed possession of de Belmaison and his companions.

"They claim to be in the service of Christ, yet he said that about my child!" Anastasia moaned as soon as they were safely clear of the building.

"I know," Evgenos muttered grimly, for he had been well taught since his arrival about the dangers of the Evil Eye. "And look at what the rest of them are getting up to!" He pointed toward the shore.

There, for all the local people could do to interfere—and they were being laughed at, or threatened, for their pains—the men from the ships which now rode at anchor in the bay had built a great fire, using whatever they could find that would burn. Not only had they taken the village's stock of driftwood, in itself precious on an island with so few trees; those of them who possessed maces or axes had also attacked the barrels destined for this year's wine and oil, and even the hull of the Kaloyiannis family's boat, retrieved at the cost of so much effort after its side had been stove in against a rock in the last gale.

Four or five of them were bloodying the sand as they hung up the slaughtered pig to drain on a pole. Even while Evgenos and Anastasia watched in horror, they gashed its belly to let out the inwards, which they promptly tossed aside. Were they insane? Why waste so much good food? It was awful to think of the sausages it would have made!

Dogs had been brought ashore, too: hulking but ill-favored beasts that had to be kept at bay with whips. One of the soldiers, grinning satanically, used his on the wife of the pig's owner, who was begging for at least the offal, and to emphasize his point caught up a handful of the guts and hurled them as far as he could. Instantly the dogs converged on them and began to fight, which amused the soldiers hugely. The woman, a lash mark reddening across her cheek, turned away howling louder than the dogs.

Meantime the goose and chickens were being roughly plucked and cleaned, then spitted on whatever sticks had not yet been thrown into the fire.

Laughing and joking, more of the soldiers—there must be thirty-five or forty of them altogether, Evgenos estimated—appeared carrying all the barrels and skin bottles of wine that they could find. At once they were the center of their comrades' attention, and most of what was left from last year's vintage was promptly spilled either down their gullets or on the ground: either way, gone to waste.

Then someone reported his discovery of the baker's, its oven containing not only new bread but also the stews and other dishes the better-off families had taken there to be cooked during divine service. To the utter horror of the onlookers, the soldiers instantly forgot about the pig and the poultry, leaving them to char for want of being turned, and seized on this new discovery, emptying the earthenware pots so fast they nearly choked themselves, then hurling them to smash on the rocky ground. Whenever anybody tried to stop them, they cursed and struck out, drunkenly now, sometimes only with fists, but more than once with weapons. The middle Kaloyiannis boy, braver or angrier than most, was rewarded with a gash across his thigh which felled him to the ground, and the man who had delivered the blow was restrained with difficulty from chopping at him again.

Aghast in the doorway of the church, the *papas* shouted at de Belmaison, demanding why he was letting his men behave worse than pagans or Mussulmen. But, grinning cynically, the French lord and three of his companions ignored his complaints and went to claim a share of the spoils, each ordering his followers to bring him the choicest food and drink. The priest burst into unashamed sobs.

"How can Christians act this way?" he screamed.

The one-eyed man, who had remained in the shadow of the church door, emerged blinking into sunlight and laid a consolatory hand on his arm. In his stilted Greek he said, "They have been disappointed in their hope of fighting the Saracens. We should have reached the Holy Land a month ago. When it is ours again, you will be amply repaid for what they're taking."

A little reassured, the *papas* wiped away his tears. Anastasia, however, still frightened because the one-eyed man might, wittingly or unwittingly, have ill-wished her unborn child, clutched at Evgenos's arm, whimpering.

"Yes, let's make ourselves scarce," the latter muttered. "Any moment now these devils are going to remember there are women here, and my guess is they've had to manage without any for quite some time. Of course, they will have used the boys instead, but even so . . . And some of them are loathsomely diseased. We'd better make for home and hope against hope that they'll be too drunk to think about exploring the whole island before they leave."

Anastasia's face twisted in horror, and despite her condition she followed him homeward at a frantic run.

Having penned their chickens in the cave above their hut, and hidden the rest of their few possessions as best they could, they waited tensely throughout an afternoon that dragged on unendurably. Apart from the humming of bees, and as evening drew on the clicking of cicadas, there was almost no sound; yet they often fancied they could hear a scream from the direction of the village, or a harsh cruel laugh, or the echo of yet another pot or dish being casually broken by those who would be gone tomorrow, heedless of how long it would take the islanders to repair their meager fortunes.

Even after sunset, though he allowed Anastasia to go and lie down, Evgenos did not relax his vigilance. Armed with a heavy olive branch by way of a club, he sat amid the gathering darkness, daring to dream that he, sober, might be a match for any number of soldiers fuddled with drink. Yet his belly growled, and the acid taste of hunger rose in his mouth as he thought of the good food the invaders had gobbled down or tossed aside. He hadn't eaten meat in weeks, not since their oldest hen became too old to lay.

It grew very late. He had almost allowed himself the luxury of imagining that, here at the distant southern tip of Oragalia, they were destined to escape the predations of the crusaders, when he caught the noise of someone slipping on the steep and pebbly path across the headland, followed by a curse and a chuckle—the latter, no doubt from someone else. So there were going to be at least two of them. Cautiously, noiselessly, he crawled into concealment among bushes so dry it cost him all his self-control to prevent their twigs from snapping. Tonight the moon was almost at its full; he could see a long way. He would be well prepared when they got here.

He wondered whether to waken Anastasia, but decided against it. Best if she slept the sleep of exhaustion. Of course, if he failed in his defense of her—

But he refused to let himself entertain the idea.

Nonetheless his feigned confidence waned when he first caught a glimpse of the men heading toward him. One of the pair appeared to be a giant, with shoulders as wide as the church door! Then he realized his mistake. That was two men, both of ordinary size, supporting one another and their common burden of a clumsy ancient pottery wine jar against the rough going. A pang of relief transfixed him—only to vanish as he realized: not two men coming his way, but three.

He sought what consolation he could in the fact that they were definitely common soldiery. They carried no shields; hence probably they did not possess swords either, although they doubtless had clubs or knives, and what passed for their armor would be nothing more than padded leather. One accurate blow to each of their heads, with all the violence at his command, and . . .

But that was wishful thinking. He drove himself to the utmost pitch of concentration, and realized he was going to have to let them pass, on their way to where Anastasia lay, in order to attack them from behind. Whether they were drunk or sober, it was too risky to confront them.

They drew level with him, cursing and complaining in a tongue he did not understand, though he could well guess what two of them were saying to the third: "It had better be worth coming all this way!" Holding his breath, he waited until their backs were turned, and poised to leap down with his improvised weapon swinging. And at that very instant there came the sound of other, hastier, footsteps, and a sharp voice raised as though issuing an order.

He was too tense to work out the implications of that. All he could think of was that there were now four men to contend with, and the three he had been about to attack were just on the point of turning around—

I should have been praying while I waited, Evgenos grieved to himself, and launched his onslaught with a yell.

As well as surprise, he had the advantage of knowing every inch of this end of the island, but even so he was too late to take the trio completely aback. As befitted good soldiers—which in the proper circumstances they might be—they responded with reflex speed, heedless of the antiquity of the jar they carried, and the more important fact that it was still half-full. It fell to the ground and smashed, and gave him an extra precious second to take aim, for the liquid made their footing instantly slippery, and they almost lost their balance.

This stroke of luck provided Evgenos with time to crack the nearest of them over the head with all his might and knock him unconscious, but before his victim had measured his length the other two were charging, and it was sheer luck that enabled him to swipe them both, painfully, before having to retreat with his back against the rock. His breath rasped in his throat; the air was horribly dry and full of dust.

From the direction of the path came another shout, full of menace. He had no time to think about that, though. He was compelled to hurl his club first this way, then that, with hands so slippery with sweat (and how could that be, when the air was so dry?) that he risked losing his grip. One or two of his blows connected; the rest were near enough to make his opponents jump aside and regroup. But those which did hit home seemed not to do any harm, and pretty soon one of the soldiers was going to hit him, maybe on the arm or hand, and there was yet another shout from behind, this time loud and angry, and—*missed me, by a miracle! Help me, saints! You can't let these brutes rape Anastasia! You can't! Yet here they are coming at me again, and the one that I knocked flying is struggling to his feet, and I'm tiring already because it's so long since I filled my belly with such good food as they stole from us today, and I hear the other one coming up behind me, closer and closer— Got you, you spawn of Satan!*

Fair and square on the cheek, and I felt his teeth go crunch, and there he is tripping over his own feet but here come the others both at once—Help me, St. Michael and St. George, the dragon killers! Because if you don't . . .

Oh, Lord God Almighty. We've woken Anastasia, and I can see her coming out of the hut, and—

The world spun. He had tripped on a loose pebble and been clubbed on the right shoulder, both at once. The shock ran like a lightning bolt clear to the tips of his fingers, and while he was struggling to recover he heard a shout so close behind him he felt convinced he was about to die. Somehow they had lured him away from the rock that had protected his back at the beginning, so as to give the fourth of them an opening . . .

"Stand aside!"

And he was rudely thrust off balance. He went sprawling in dirt churned up to mud, his nose and lungs full of the stench of warm sour wine, as harsh as vomit. Moaning in terror, he rolled over, clinging to his club, and discovered that all his latest guesses had been wrong. This newcomer was not bent on the same errand as the others. Moreover he had a sword and shield, and he knew Greek, though he was speaking another language now, and furiously.

It was the one-eyed knight.

For a space the three soldiers seemed minded to defy him, but he clouted the foremost of them soundly with the flat of his sword and then presented its point under the man's chin, still uttering a torrent of obvious abuse. The spirit went out of them. Sullenly they obeyed his command to wend their way back to the village, although they kept muttering complaints until they were out of earshot.

"Sir!" Evgenos dropped to one knee. "Sir, I owe you my life! And as for Anastasia—" She had come to join him, realizing the danger was past, and he caught her hand.

But the right words refused to pass his lips.

Kicking aside fragments of the wine jar as he sheathed his sword, the one-eyed man said, "It was my duty as a Christian to frustrate de Belmaison's intentions. Oh, get up, man! You're no liege of mine."

"But I owe you my life!" Evgenos repeated.

The knight's lip curled into a cynical grin, half-concealed by his scruffy beard. "I'm not so sure of that, even. You seemed to be giving a pretty good account of yourself. As a matter of fact, there have been times on the field of battle when I'd have been glad of a squire as stout as you!"

Anastasia flinched, thinking for a second he meant to enlist Evgenos. The knight noticed, and interpreted her reaction accurately.

"Ah, don't worry. I have my own retainers, and they are better disciplined than de Belmaison's."

"It was he who sent those three to? . . ."

"Yes indeed. He has no control over his baser

appetites. That's why I set out after them, as soon as I discovered the sort of errand they were on. He'd told them to locate 'the blackamoor's woman'"—a nod at Anastasia—"and drag you back for his enjoyment. It was indicated that if they took advantage of you on the way, he'd not object."

In horror Anastasia whispered, "And these are the folk who plan to liberate the Holy Land?"

"I think they won't," the knight replied, his voice betraying sudden weariness. He dropped the point of his shield to the ground and leaned on it. "But you must not judge us all by the actions of a few: particularly not by de Belmaison's. He belongs to no knightly Order, he has taken no oaths except an oath of fealty to his king, and there is little to choose between him and his crude peasant followers. Myself, on the other hand . . . Ah, but it's enough to have done the proper thing. I'll bid you good night."

"Wait, sir, if you please!" Anastasia darted forward. "I wish to know who you are and why you helped us, if only to remember you forever in my prayers!"

"Yes! Yes!" exclaimed Evgenos fervently, regaining his feet at last.

The knight gave a sad and cynical chuckle. "Well, here's a change in the wind! At noon you were prepared to imagine I had cast the Evil Eye upon your child—is that not so?"

"I beg your honor's forgiveness!" Anastasia cried.

"Don't let your soul be troubled by it. I was unaware of the beliefs that rule your people, or I'd not have made so bold . . . I'll answer you as honestly as I can, then, although my name's of no account. I lost my lands and family long ago. There was a plague. Still, for the sake of my Order, I'll say this.

"The Order of the Knights Hospitalers was founded to tend those injured in the service of the Cross. It is no longer what it used to be, and there are many who profane its binding oath. You can identify me in your prayers as one—and possibly the only one—who absolutely won't!"

On which he caught up his shield and strode away. Evgenos made to run after, but Anastasia checked him.

"You heard what he said! It shames him to admit what depths his comrades can descend to. Don't force him to think of them again. Praise God, rather, that some few righteous men are still alive!"

Later:

"Gene?" she whispered into the dark.

"Oh, I'm not asleep, Stacy. Even though it must be midnight. I don't imagine I shall sleep. I can't rid my mind of the image of de Belmaison—smug, self-righteous, prepared to condone the worst excesses because he's so totally convinced his cause is just!"

"No, you should think rather of the one-eyed man, and Hedwig too."

"Him, yes of course—but why her, for pity's sake?"

"Because he got it right, she got it wrong."

"I don't quite follow."

"Oh, you know Hedwig . . . I don't mean that; I mean: you know about her."

"Yes, but—"

"Let me explain, then. She was self-sacrificing, wasn't she? She was the self-sacrificial type *par excellence*, and viewed herself as an embodiment of altruism. However, this wasn't quite the way she struck other people, caught up as they were in the fulfillment of her ambition like leaves being whirled along in the wake of a fast car."

He found the resources for a laugh. "Oh, yes! Oh, very yes! But what became of her? Tell me!"

"The world she found her way to was a compendium of the wrongs she sought to right. Where there was not a brutal overlord enslaving the innocent, there was a plague; where not a famine, then greedy tax collectors; where not a drought, then war and all its countless victims, specially children. She was in her element, and she reveled in it!

"Promptly she began to organize reforms, and hordes of people flocked to support her projects. Naturally, being a visitor from far away, she enjoyed an automatic cachet. Think of any artist immigrating from abroad as a parallel; think, for instance, how many composers and musicians had to seek their fame in foreign countries.

"And in a sense she *was* an artist—a specialist, at all events—and here she was supplied with more material to work on than she'd ever dared to dream of. For a long while she was happy. She was deliriously happy."

"But what became of her in the end?" Gene murmured sleepily.

"I think you might well guess. Come on! You said you weren't likely to fall asleep tonight."

He rolled over, eyes closed. "I may well have been wrong about that . . . Uh—yes! Hedwig! Like you said, she reached the sort of world she'd always dreamed of."

"*And*—?" She prompted him with a nudge.

"Oh! It could never run short of causes for her to dedicate herself to. There were always going to be worse things in the news tomorrow than the ones she had set out to cure today. Is that how you see her fate?"

"It turned out worse," Stacy countered. "In fact she won, insofar as she cleansed the world of the evils that she found on her arrival. But ultimately she found herself obliged to organize yet one more project on top of all the rest: a campaign to provide charity for the people she'd inspired, those who, as a result of copying her example, found they had lost everything they cared about—their homes, their families, their loved ones, their heirlooms and their other prized possessions . . . To this end, of course, she had to recruit still further helpers, or perhaps one might better term them worshipers, who in turn complained about what they'd had to abandon at her behest. Finally it dawned on her that here was one campaign without an end. She who had so consistently sacrificed herself had paid no heed to the other people she was spending as the price of her achievements. Her conscience rebelled, but the fact remained: she had incurred one debt she never could repay . . . Gene? *Gene?*"

But he was asleep. A moment later, so was she.

7

THE EXHIBIT

consists in the fragments of a jar that once held wine.
It can never be made whole again

THE MONTH

is October

THE NAME

is Pedro

NIKODEMOS, NICKNAMED CHRYSOCHEIROS "OF THE golden hand" owing to the success that usually attended his business ventures, was furious with himself, and even angrier with God. His usual combination of luck and good judgment had utterly deserted him. What should have been the most profitable voyage even he had ever undertaken risked turning out to be an unqualified disaster.

Taking advantage of the exceptionally early advent of the west-to-east trade winds this year—they had shifted exactly at the Equinox, instead of lagging—a handful of bold or greedy Indian traders had set sail weeks ahead of their normal schedule, determined to beat their rivals to Egypt. Their gold and pearls and precious stones could be sold at leisure, but whoever arrived first with seasonal and perishable goods, such as perfumes, incense, spices and dyestuffs, was sure of commanding the highest prices. That was a principle which Nikodemos understood well. His agents on the Red Sea had standing instructions to buy as soon as the traders showed up each year, provided their merchandise was of sound quality, and forward the goods overland to Alexandria as fast as possible. To bring the winter's first shipload of Indian luxuries to Constantinople, in addition to the regular Egyptian exports of linen, pottery, glassware and papyrus—not that papyrus was so much in demand anymore—implied a huge commercial killing. Declining though that city's fortunes were, its inhabitants were determined to make the most of this life rather than rely on the promise of a paradise to come.

But this year the early arrival of Indian goods had taken even Nikodemos by surprise. On the day when a warning message was brought to him from the south, his best ship was still in dock, being recaulked and rerigged, and apart from his African shipmaster, known as Porias because only a barbarian could pronounce his proper name, most of the crew who regularly signed with him were still making ends meet in the tourist trade. Those few wealthy families who could afford a summer visit to relatives on Crete or Cyprus preferred, as did Nikodemos himself, seamen with plenty of experience.

Frantic orders, messages dispatched with small hope of reaching their recipients, and the squandering of far too much ready cash, had resulted in him putting his ship to sea well ahead of his chief rival and sworn personal enemy, Kranes. But the latter had stood on the quay and shouted insults as she was being readied for departure.

"What a bunch of water rats you've had to make do with! They'll eat your cargo before you get to any port where you can sell it! *If* you reach port, and I'm inclined to doubt it—look at your sheets, look at your sails! Hah! You'll founder before you're out of sight of land!"

Enraged beyond bearing, Nikodemos had retorted, "I wouldn't bet on it if I were you!"

"You're in the mood to wager? Very well, I'll match you! I have a sounder ship that's being loaded right now with richer cargo, and I have a better crew as well. Even if we leave a day—no, make that three days—later than you, I'd still expect to beat you to Constantinople!"

"Never!"

"I'll stake my entire cargo, and the ship into the bargain, and these people on the dockside are my witnesses! Will you do the same?"

Recklessly Nikodemos bellowed, "Yes, of course!"

Then Kranes sprang his trap. "Very well! I brought my clerk along, and he's been writing down our words, yours as well as mine. As soon as you're at sea, I'll have copies posted all over Alexandria. Either you'll be a poor man when you return, or you won't dare to, and you'll have to eke out the rest of your miserable life as a bankrupt exile!"

Chortling with glee, he turned away, and Nikodemos gave the order to cast off.

Fuming!

It was because of Kranes's arrogance, and not because of the profit he stood to lose—or so he was now insisting to Porias—that, after making the usual landfall on the eastern cape of Crete, he had insisted on an unfamiliar route among the treacherous islands north of there. Their *periplus* advised against it, but he scoffed, and with a heavy heart Porias obeyed him. Was it his fault—Nikodemos was now demanding of heaven—was it his fault that a gale sprang up an hour after they left Crete astern? Did he command the weather, or did God? In the latter case God must be on the side of Kranes, and that was absurd! He was a drunkard, a lecher, and a notorious cheat!

All of which most signally failed to impress Porias or any other of the crew when, around the middle of a moonless night, they found themselves being driven even with their sail furled toward an island that showed on the horizon as a featureless black outline. Sometimes its silhouette seemed to resemble a crouching beast, but the impression never lasted long enough for them to figure out what kind.

Seasick—he who was so proud of never having thrown up in the worst of storms—and terrified of losing not just the ship and her cargo, but even his chance of paying off a lost bet with aplomb—he who boasted of never having defaulted on a business deal—Nikodemos clung to the rigging in wild wet darkness and blasphemed.

A rock loomed up. There were screams and near panic, but Porias tongue-lashed his men into action and they fended it off with poles. One broke, and the man wielding it vanished overboard with a howl. Yet the ship survived, and a moment later sank her bow safely into a sandbank. Her hull, miraculously, remained intact.

But the shock was too great for her already weakened rigging, and ropes began to snap with a noise like cracking whips. Snaking down to deck level, they caught two of the crewmen, one around the body and the other around the leg, and flung them off their feet. The mast tilted; the wind tore loose one end of the sail and the yard canted down far enough on the port side to strike another man violently on the head. Porias bellowed more orders, and the crew sullenly obeyed them. But when a semblance of normality had been restored, and they had a chance to take stock, they found that one man had a wrenched knee and another a dislocated arm, while the one who had been cracked on the pate was out of his wits; all he could do was clutch his neck and moan, his mouth hideously ajar.

"What are we going to do?" Nikodemos whimpered.

"Wait for daylight—what else?" said Porias with African contempt, and lay down where he was and fell asleep.

Something strange and terrifying was happening to Anastasia. Evgenos was bewildered by it, and wished he could appeal to the wise women of Oragalia for information—but for the most part they refused to have anything to do with him. Had they not watched Anastasia grow up they would have rejected her just as completely. However, a trace of sympathy lingered for the girl who had been orphaned at so early an age, and now and then one of them left a gift anonymously at the peak of the path leading down to the cove and cave where they eked out their existence: a loaf, some figs, a fish or a head of garlic—bribes intended to make her reject him so she could be welcomed into the respectable company of widowhood. There were many widows on the island younger than she was.

There would be no gift tonight, not with the wind howling across the sea and chasing giant waves up the beach. Why had she chosen now—now of all times, and in her condition—to go clambering around the headland in search of mussels, which she ate raw, forcing their shells apart with her teeth regardless of the way it chipped them. Lately she had complained so often of toothache!

And small wonder. Was there not a saying that women paid with teeth for babies' bones?

Now he must go out again in the pitch blackness, coax her back, comfort her as best he could against the terrible demands of the new life growing in her womb . . .

Resignedly, thankful that it was not actually raining, he fought his way against the gale to where she sat cramming her belly. Dropping to his knees at her side, he demanded, "What's amiss?"

"I'm hungry," was her sullen reply. Then, apologetically, she added, "It isn't *just* hunger. I'm hungry for something special—something that isn't bread, that isn't fruit, that isn't eggs . . . Oh, I don't know what it is!"

His heart sank. Last time she had demanded goat cheese, and they had no goat of their own, so he had had to spend a day working for a master who hated him, and in the evening taken home his pay: two big handfuls of feta. And she had tasted and refused it, saying it was wrong.

Wrong? How could cheese be wrong? It had tasted all right to him. But pregnant women were notorious for their weird behavior . . .

Abruptly she broke down crying, and had to spit out the last mussel she had taken into her mouth. He led her back up to the cave, muttering vague words of reassurance, and tasted sea salt on her lips before she fell asleep despite the roaring and yelling of the wind, sprawled on the moist and rotten softness of the seaweed he had gathered to make them a bed.

He, however, lay wakeful for a good while yet, wondering what devil had condemned him to this foreign shore. But even though he desperately wanted to, he knew he could no longer leave it. He had created a responsibility for himself. Of course, giving birth was a dangerous event. Anastasia and the child might die. Then he could choose to starve or flee. However, he was ashamed of himself for hoping that that might come to pass.

Eventually he too drowsed.

And was awoken by a shout from the cave's entrance.

Rousing all of a piece, on his feet almost before his eyes were open, registering that the storm had died down, he found himself confronted by a stranger as dark as himself: certainly no Oragalian. Short and stocky, he was clad in a linen tunic stiff with salt, belted and bordered with leather bands; also his feet were shod with leather. A stir of envy was the first thing Evgenos felt when he came to himself.

But behind him was a fat and fussy fellow in even more expensive garb, including a border on his robe dyed with Tyrian purple. However, it had run disgracefully, proof that he must have bought it from a seller who used cheap mordants.

The latter said, "Is there anybody here except you? I have to get my ship afloat again at once!"

Anastasia was awake too, now. Registering the presence of the strangers, she whimpered and rolled into the darkest corner of the cave.

"I'm Shipmaster Porias," said the African. "This is my employer, Nikodemos of Alexandria. Tell your woman to calm down. All we want is help in freeing our ship from the sandbank she's stuck on. We're shorthanded because we lost a man overside in last night's gale and three more are badly hurt. We'll pay you well. But is there anyone here apart from you and the girl?"

"N-no!" At the promise of pay Evgenos found his tongue. "But—uh—I'll do what I can! What ship?"

"Wipe your eyes and you'll see her plain enough!" was Porias's curt reply.

The fat man babbled something about delay. Evgenos ignored him and pushed past into daylight.

And there she was: grounded on the bar guarding the southern bay of Oragalia, which had ensured that this patch of salt-sour ground had never been claimed by anyone until Evgenos and Anastasia were driven to try and scrape their living off it. His practiced eye informed him that she was already starting to lift clear of the entrapping sand.

He wanted to laugh, but dared not. Why, here was his chance to escape for good and all! If he told these strangers he'd help, but his price was a place in their crew . . .

Behind him Anastasia was rising to her feet. He sighed and changed his mind. He had ordained his own doom.

"The wind will turn after midday," he said dully. "By then you should have been able to shovel away enough of the sand to free her bow. Now leave us in peace."

"No! Wait!" Unpredictable as ever, Anastasia was at his side, smoothing down the calf-long black dress which she had slept in because it was her only garment. Brushing back her thick and tangled hair, she smiled at Porias and Nikodemos with all the expertise of a coquette, heedless of her chipped front teeth.

"Evgenos will help you, of course! Won't you?"—with a meaning glare. "But what cargo does your ship carry?"

"You want to buy something?" Instantly Nikodemos's commercial instincts were alerted.

Porias snorted and turned away, his posture asking more clearly than words: *What could these poverty-stricken folk afford from you?*

Anastasia, though, advanced on Nikodemos, hands outstretched, her eyes huge and pleading and full of tears.

"Yes, I do! I so much want—!"

She checked, frightened by the intensity of her desires.

"Well then, what?" Nikodemos snapped. "Just ask!"

"Some—some sort of food that I can't name!"

"Lord have mercy!" Nikodemos glanced at the sun. "By this time Kranes must be well out to sea, and he'll have avoided last night's gale, and—Porias, can you make these people see sense? We may have to dump some of the deck cargo to lighten the ship and float her off! Think that might satisfy them?"

"And what use would they have here for linens and papyrus?" Porias returned with a scowl.

"The linens only weigh heavy because a wave soaked them last night—"

"I don't want linen!" Anastasia cried. "I don't want—whatever the other thing was you mentioned! I want food for my baby! I want something I can feel, but I can't name!"

Moaning, she clenched her fists before her face.

"Oh, for the love of heaven! I'll pay your man with a jar of Indian pepper, how about that? I'll wager that's something you've never tasted! Or a pot of honey, which they say is good for pregnant women! Just so long as he works hard and honestly and comes with us now, at once!" Nikodemos was almost dancing up and down with rage and frustration.

"Take the honey," Evgenos suggested with a sigh, turning in search of his buskins.

"No, we have honey—there are lots of bees on the island! I want . . ." She bit her lip, considering. "Maybe I do want pepper; I don't know. Is it good nourishing food that fills the belly and drives away the kind of hunger you can't name?"

"No, it's a spice that fills the mouth and disguises the flavor of bad meat!" Porias snapped. "And I imagine you don't get much of that, good or bad! Your man's right—you should take the honey. Or a jar of wine, or . . . Wait: we have Egyptian waterfowl preserved in their own grease, a delicacy!"

Anastasia's eyes lightened. But Nikodemos interrupted before she could speak again.

"Not those! They're a very special item, and they'll sell for—"

"Do you want the ship refloated?" Porias flared. "Or do you want to keep the stuff and sell it at a loss when we get to Constantinople? Not that it'll be yours to sell by then, come to think of it, not if Kranes beats us. You know what sort of person he is! He'll have armed men stationed on the quayside to seize our cargo, and he'll have bribed the port police to make certain we don't try and stop them! Do you look forward to spending the winter in jail?"

"Very well," said Nikodemos sullenly. "But one jar, mind!"

"And one of honey, and one of wine!" Evgenos insisted.

"It's a deal," Porias said promptly. "You can take it out of my share if you like, Nikodemos. But if you do, then this will be our last trip together. Let's get a move on, shall we?"

The man with the wrenched knee and the man with the dislocated arm had been borne ashore by their shipmates. Now they were sitting on their haunches in the shade cast by the bales and bundles which had been taken from the deck to lighten the ship, tending their comrade who had been hit on the head. The latter's neck was definitely fractured; he lay writhing in pain with his eyes closed. Now and then he tried to say something, but all that emerged was a moan.

Three of the crew were mending the rigging and restepping the mast. The rest were knee-deep in water, wearily plying what came to hand—poles, bits of wood, pottery shards—in their attempts to free the bow. As Evgenos came to join them they paused and looked him over sullenly.

"Well, there's a plank you can use for a shovel," Porias said, pointing. "Get to it!"

"Put my pay on shore first," said Evgenos.

"What?" Porias balled his fists, taking a step closer. "Are you saying that you doubt my word?"

"Not yours. His"—with a jerk of his thumb at Nikodemos, who had darted off to inspect his damaged goods.

"You're a shrewd bastard, aren't you?" Porias said grudgingly. "You seem to be a good judge of character, at least . . . Very well. I'll pick out the stuff myself and put it over there in the shadow of that rock, all right?"

"Right!" Evgenos answered. He seized the plank and set to with a will.

Despite his gauntness and his hollow belly, he seemed to be fitter than the seamen, and dug much faster than they did. Still, that wasn't surprising; he hadn't slaved away half of last night in the teeth of the gale. The sun climbed to the zenith, and he could no longer tell whether he was wetter from seawater than from perspiration, or the other way around. But the ship's bow was coming free.

"Thirsty?"

And to his surprise, here was Porias with a pottery vase of water on a rope sling, going from man to man and allowing each three mouthfuls, neither more nor less. Wiping the sweat from his eyes after gulping down his share, Evgenos said, "When that's empty, go find Anastasia. Ask her to show you the spring we use. It runs slow at the end of summer, but it's good and sweet."

The prospect of plenty of water for the next leg of the trip cheered the seamen, and they began to look on Evgenos with less jaundiced eyes.

The sun slanted downward. The mast was secure again and the rigging, though lumpy with knots, was back to usable condition. Evgenos paused, waiting for the first hint of an offshore breeze. As soon as it came, he tossed his plank aboard the ship and turned to Porias.

"Unfurl your sail and get everyone here to shove her off. She'll move now."

Before complying, the shipmaster looked him over

curiously. He said, "You seem to know something about ships and the sea. Did you learn it on your way here?"

For an instant memory flared, of a voyage infinitely longer and stranger than any Porias or his master could have undertaken. But there were no words to cast his story in, and anyway nobody would have believed him. Evgenos settled for a grunted, "Yes!"

"So were you—? No, I sense you prefer not to talk about it. Your pay is on the beach, anyway. I hope your girl enjoys it. Now where in heaven's name is my boss?"

"He's on board," someone muttered. "Said he couldn't stand the heat and had to go below."

"That's added a few more talents' weight to the load we have to shift," Porias sighed. "I think I'll make this my last trip with him whether he loses his bet with Kranes or not . . . Right, men! Yare now, yare! Set your shoulders to the bow and push!"

And after a lot of slipping and sliding on the loose bottom, they forced the boat clear. Hanging on to a cable along with four of the seamen for fear she might adrift, Porias shouted at Evgenos.

"Don't suppose you'd care to ship with us, would you? We could use an extra hand as smart as you!"

Last night Evgenos had been dreaming of a chance to quit this island where everybody seemed to hate him except Anastasia . . . and sometimes lately he hadn't been quite sure about her. But if he accepted this invitation, when he came back he could count on one thing beyond a doubt: she would have been turned into a widow even though she wasn't one. Even if she and the baby survived, he would be a complete outcast. And he had been an outcast before he found his way to Oragalia . . .

Would these men accept him as one of themselves, let him make a career as part of this ship's crew? More likely they'd be glad to see the back of him once the voyage was over and they had no more use for his services. Besides, he had gathered that Nikodemos stood to lose ship and cargo too if he arrived late at Constantinople. Then he'd be stranded further from home than ever, and moreover in a great city. He had no experience of cities, but he had been warned that a man could feel more alone in a vast crowd than by himself in the middle of a desert or an ocean. It was better to be reluctantly tolerated on Oragalia than to endure that kind of bitter loneliness.

On top of all of which there was Anastasia, and soon there would be the child too—his first . . .

He forced a smile, shook his head, and shouted back.

"Thank you, Shipmaster! But I've made a life here!" The double meaning of the phrase startled him for a second; it had been unpremeditated. "I wish you a swift safe trip from now on, anyhow!"

"It's a kind thought! I'm obliged!"

The men were making haste to climb aboard, carrying their injured shipmates on their shoulders through the shallows. Nikodemos had reappeared and was shouting something about retrieving the goods that had been dumped on shore, but nobody seemed to be paying him much heed.

Nor Evgenos. Despondently he turned away to collect the preserved Egyptian waterfowl, the wine and the honey. His mind filled with miserable second thoughts: could he not have demanded more, much more? And was he right after all in declining to leave the island? Life was harsher here, in some senses, than at sea, and there were people who praised great cities despite their drawbacks . . .

But here was Anastasia coming to meet him. Her eyes grew wide as she looked not at what he was carrying but at the abandoned cargo.

"They left all that behind? Oh, you can take it to the village and people will pay us well for it! It's cloth, isn't it?"

"Did you guide Porias to the spring?" Evgenos asked, abruptly aware how tired his long hot morning's work had made him; he looked forward to sampling the wine, above all.

"Yes!" She started. "Was that wrong?"

"No, I suggested it. They weren't bad people, you know. They could have beaten me into working for them, couldn't they? Then, of course, I wouldn't have worked half so hard . . . What am I talking about? Let's get home. I'm dreadfully hot and thirsty, and half-starved."

"But oughtn't you to bring all that stuff to the cave right away? Suppose somebody else—"

"Who? Who ever comes this way, except some of your relatives by stealth, at night?"

"I'll bring it, then!"

"No! You work too hard anyhow for a woman in your condition—"

"I have to, don't I? If I didn't—"

He forced himself to remain calm, but interrupted nonetheless.

"I'll bring everything up to the cave before sundown, and later I'll carry it to the village and sell it as you recommend. But there are some folk on this island who might try to steal it, aren't there? We'll have to be careful about how much we admit to having. And I'm too tired to make plans right now."

He feared for a moment that she was going to argue; he added hastily, "Besides, what I have here is exactly what you've been saying you want. Let's sample it."

Yielding, she reached out to relieve him of part of his load.

The instant the seals on the jars were broken, the still air of the cave was filled with the most delectable aroma. With a cry of joy Anastasia drew out and devoured one after another of the potted birds, using for want of a better dish to save them from the sand a tile he had found that bore a scratched inscription in a language neither of them could read. With immense relief Evgenos relaxed, taking only token portions for himself until she decided to tackle the honey instead. Like the wine, it was exceptional, far richer than any made on Oragalia.

Discovering the fact, she calmed and set the rest of the jar aside.

"If I eat more, I shall make myself ill," she sighed. "I shall take a little every day, but only a little, until it's gone. It will be for the sake of our child. Such sweetness cannot but do him good."

Evgenos was leaning back contentedly against the rocky wall. Hard work, wine and good food were combining to make him drowsy. Leaning toward him, she tapped his knee.

"It's nearly sundown, and you did say you'd bring the other things up here!"

Grumpy, but resigned, he forced himself to his feet and went to keep his promise.

There were eight big bales altogether, each as much of a load as he could manage because they were still soaked with seawater. Five were of fine linen, a great prize. The others, he guessed, might be of papyrus, for which he foresaw small demand on the island. Perhaps, though, the priest or the lawyer might find a use for it, and in any case if he left it in the open it would certainly draw the attention of would-be thieves.

Having set the bales where they would dry most quickly, he returned to Anastasia and found her dozing. At his touch, however, she stirred, and said with her eyes still closed, "Those men made me think of Pedro, you know."

Yawning, stretching, preparing to lie down beside her in the gathering dark, he said, "How do you mean?"

"Was he not a trader to his very bones, yet not content with ordinary goods? Would he not always set the highest store by what was marvelous and strange, and did he not expect everybody else to feel the same?"

"Go on."

Sleepily, she did so.

"The world he lusted to find a way to, then, must have been a place of wonders so far exceeding the normal run of our experience as to defy description. Were there foods? Then they must transcend ambrosia. Were there cloths and fabrics? Then they must be softer than a morning breeze and warmer than the summer sun. Were there dyes? Then their colors must be such as never yet graced any rainbow. Were there furs? Then they must retain the life of the beasts that yielded them, caressing and conforming to the bodies of their wearers. Were there drugs? Then they must not only cure the regular diseases, but instantly confer such gaiety and vigor as never any did in the drab world he left behind!"

"Yes, that's the sort of place which would suit Pedro. So he found it?"

"It's . . . necessary to believe he did."

"And no doubt"—Evgenos rolled to embrace her, licking mingled fat and honey on her cheek—"he dreamed of making his fortune out of it."

"Not one fortune. A thousand. There was no end to the strangeness of that place. Eagerly he settled down to send home a report . . . and could not even draft one. Gene, are you paying attention?"

"Yes, yes!"—amid the tresses of her hair. "Why could he not make out his report?"

"The world was truly unfamiliar. So it did indeed defy description."

8

THE EXHIBIT

is a graffito on a red clay tile, scarcely legible.
It marks the desperate need of somebody to be remembered

THE MONTH

is November

THE NAME

is Naruhiko

SEVEN YEARS AGO, ONE OF THE ARROGANT AND vainglorious Romans who now ruled the Middle Sea had found his way to the otherwise unimportant island of Oragalia, and decided to turn it into his private estate, calculating that he could make it self-sufficient if he introduced modern methods of farming and irrigation. He had also intended to build a villa in the Italian style, centered around an atrium with a fountain as fine as any at Pompeii. But the marble and mosaic which he dreamed of cost too much, and he died before his overambitious project was completed.

Almost the only relic of his intrusion was a channel which brought fresh water down from hillside springs to the miniature forum of the town that had developed beside the eastern bay. There it was fed first into a stone trough, for drinking and cooking, and the citizens came and went from dawn to dusk with jars and skin bottles to be filled. Lower down, it trickled into a wide basin, and this was used to water livestock, and for laundry. Families rich enough to own a slave or two, but not a private water supply, sent them thither most days, and they behaved as bossily as their owners, insisting on priority over every other would-be user. Because the alternative was to beat their clothes in seawater and spread them to dry on the rocks of the shore—treatment that wore the fabric out in next to no time—the poorer sort generally deferred to them, hanging back until the basin was foul with grease and masses of shed fiber clogged the outflow, whereupon they had to set to and clear the mess away with their bare hands. Sometimes the delay could cost them half a precious day.

The only person among them who defied this obsequious custom was Anastasia. She who had little of her own to wash, since her adopted kinfolk had been stolen into slavery, mocked these other slaves when she arrived with laundry belonging to those who could afford—and dared—to rent her time, elbowed her way to the cleanest part of the pool, and kept up a constant flow of muttered insults concerning cowards who let themselves be bought and sold instead of running away to earn an independent living.

Poor though she was even by the standards of a poverty-stricken community, having been orphaned at birth and worse than orphaned in her teens, she was never in rags, for she often took her pay in outworn garments and painstakingly repaired them; moreover, despite being gaunt she was beautiful, with brilliant dark eyes and long sleek hair. The occasional strangers who noticed her invariably demanded why she was neither married nor enrolled in the household of a prosperous family, but the islanders were ashamed to explain why nobody dared lay a finger on her, and dodged the question. Even though the forum was beset with crude statues of gods and goddesses, both local and imposed by the Romans, and the whole island was littered with shrines and sacred places, admitting the truth would smack too much of superstition to a sophisticated visitor from Italy, the Greek mainland or Asia Minor. So they did their best to convey the vague impression that she was a harlot, but it was wiser not to have commerce with her because she was diseased, and then pointedly changed the subject.

None of this was true. In fact she was a witch.

Every man on the island, bond or free, who did not prefer boys to women, had lusted after her since long before she was left to fend for herself upon the enslavement of her uncle and older cousins. One of the Roman contractors brought in by the island's temporary overlord, infuriated on realizing that he was not going to be paid for the work he had put in, had sought some other form of recompense. Anastasia's uncle, who had adopted her in infancy, was a skilled stone carver, and had brought up his two sons in the same trade. A richer rival, assuming that without any menfolk to protect her Anastasia would be easy prey for himself, had suggested to the Roman that he kidnap and sell the masons to recoup his losses, a proposal which the fellow eagerly fell in with.

There was of course no court of justice Anastasia could appeal to; apart from the fact that her uncle's enemy—who was still fuming because she had rebuffed his offer to take her in with a volley of the filthiest objurgations she could contrive—was now the most powerful man on the island, none of her relatives was officially a Roman citizen. Her mother and all her grandparents being dead, she turned to other cousins, of whom she had several. She received some support from them, but they were humble farmhands, lacking a profitable skill like her uncle's. They had little to offer save a bare subsistence, and that only on condition that she work at the most menial tasks.

With one exception: her great-aunt Phoebe, who was toothless and rheumatic and could not walk without a stick. But her mind was clear as a summer sky, and she remembered many of the ancient spells that could be used against people who had committed crimes yet imagined they might escape the consequences.

Anastasia's uncle's rival also had a son, whom he had likewise apprenticed to the mason's trade. The boy could pursue it no longer; he had been blinded by stone chips that flew up unaccountably beneath his chisel.

Some of the island's young men had laughed about that and gone on trying to seduce this desirable maiden. The most importunate of them was now a geck and gull himself, for he had slipped on a hill path and broken his leg; ever since, he had had to walk sidewise, like a crab. After that, people began to draw apart from Anastasia, and though they spoke politely enough on meeting, they seemed to have decided to leave her in peace.

Then, when she tamed the wild man—a feat which echoed the most ancient legend known to anybody here—and decided to bear his child in order to emphasize her contempt for all her other would-be suitors, their respect turned to awe. Some went so far as to maintain outright that one of the Old and Strong had come again, but there was much argument concerning that opinion. At all events, now she was big-bellied and thus in a condition to work still more powerful charms than before, even the randiest of the island's men had ceased to trouble her.

She was sorry that Phoebe, dead last winter, had not survived to see the full fruits of her instruction.

"A sail! A sail!"

The cry rose from the southern headland of the bay, and at once everybody forgot their work and rushed to the shore. Even Anastasia, having wrung out the garments entrusted to her by the family employing her today and laid them back neatly in her basket, wiped her hands on her woolen cloak and deigned to join the throng, although she was as ever dismayed to notice how many mothers warned their children to keep clear of her. As if she would ever harm a child too young to know what wickedness meant! Some of those mothers, on the other hand . . .

But Phoebe had warned her that she must never use her spells to afflict either the innocent, or those who lacked the power to control their own destinies. Whether the gods existed or not, magic certainly did, and its laws decreed that it would recoil against all who exploited it with neither justice nor goodwill on their side. Anastasia bestowed broad smiles on those of the children who were looking her way, and a few of them risked smiling back.

Then she turned her attention to the ship approaching harbor. She was, predictably, a Roman galley, her sail furled, her rowers bending to their oars. In the still air the sound of the drum they kept time to could already be heard, and now and then it was punctuated by the crack of their overseer's whip.

Such a ship as that had carried off Anastasia's uncle, and his sons whom she had grown to love as brothers . . .

Her mind filled with visions of losing someone who had become even more precious to her. Blinded with sudden tears, she slipped away.

"Things are terrible, and getting worse," said Septimus Julius Cornax. "Thanks to our emperor! May his guts burn worse than the bowels of Vesuvius!"

He waved his cup vaguely in the air, and a sullen slave—nothing like as well trained as what he was used to at home—took it away for refilling.

For want of anything better to do while his crew loaded such fresh provisions as were to be had on this dismal island, he had accepted a fawning invitation to lunch at the home of its "richest" citizen. Rich? Someone had to be joking! The house's *cēnātīō* was a mere terrace in the open air, sheltered by a trellis of ill-doing vines, tolerable perhaps in summer, but absurd in November. Its sole ornament was a crude statue supposedly representing an ancient deity, while the company consisted of the man's dull and pudgy wife, who luckily excused herself early, and his sightless and self-pitying son, who whined endlessly about his misfortune.

Even this, however, might have been tolerable had the food been fit for Cornax's sophisticated palate. In fact, it had proved ghastly and the wine if possible worse, so he had sent to the ship for a jar of Samian, which was now half-empty. To add to his depression, there was still no wind. His rowers would mutiny if they were ordered back to sea before tomorrow, so he was due to be stuck overnight in this armpit of the universe. In the end he grew so bored he drew his dagger and started to scratch a record of his visit on one of the crude tiles his hostess boasted about using to protect her table from the hot (meaning lukewarm) dishes set upon it. It was about then that she took the hint and made herself scarce.

By stages, however, Cornax's mood had mellowed. The sniveling son, finding the Samian too strong, had been led away, which was a vast relief. Moreover—as he admitted to himself—it was a pure delight to be able to speak his mind out of hearing of anyone who might relay his treasonable opinions to his enemies. On this lump of rock whither his ship had been driven by a contrary wind, and then becalmed unseasonably, surely there was nobody to carry back gossip to the imperial court!

Accordingly, even though he realized he was upsetting his host (but why should he care about these provincials who had nothing better to offer a distinguished guest than charred goat and a mess of onions stewed in oil?), he unleashed his tongue.

"Want to know what a plight the empire's in? Take me as an example, then! Here I am, not just entitled by descent to bear the name of the Julian *gens* but also favored with a surname that according to all the experts must date back to Etruscan times, because they can't account for it any other way—in other words, my ancestors predated the kings, let alone the emperors, of Rome!—and on top of that an officer of one of the finest of all the legions, with a roll of battle

honors going back centuries—here I am in command
of a rotten tub of a ship, on a mission that reduces me
to the status of a common or garden lanista, the kind
of person who makes money out of pandering to the
plebs, supplying them with gladiators to chop each
other's vitals off in public! Ever been to the Games in
Rome? No? I could have guessed as much. But that's
what pleases the crowd the best. There's a fad for late
eunuchs who escape the arena and survive. The
emperor likes them a *lot* . . . More wine! Come on,
you ought to have more too! It may be years before
you get another chance to taste so good a vintage!"

His host, eyes rolling every which way, declined
with tolerable politeness. Later, Cornax felt, he was
likely to reach the stage where he would regard such a
refusal as an insult, but he wasn't there yet, so he let
the matter slide, drank deeper than ever, and resumed his tirade.

"And it's bad enough knowing the slaves I collect
are going to be wasted in the arena, but that isn't the
half of it. The mob is constantly yelling for blacks, and
beastmen—ever seen one of them? No? Thought
not—and . . . Wine, you lazy scum! Or I'll call my
overseer with his whip! Excuse me; not mannerly in
someone else's house . . . But I could sell you a girl
or two—Sorry again. I'm not allowed to, and anyway
since they're bound for the court you couldn't afford
them. Where was I?"

His host, who by now was looking thoroughly
alarmed, muttered something indefinite. It was
enough to set Cornax back on course.

"Yes! Worse than being treated like a lanista is
being treated like a common merchant! 'Unguents,'
they tell me—'perfumes,' they tell me—'dormice in

honey,' they tell me—'lark tongues,' they tell me—
'Get us lots and lots so we can impress the Parthian
Ambassador!' Or the Persian one, or some other of
those foreign bigwigs! Years of effort all due to be
squandered on a single Hades-consigned banquet!
Then they're apt to chuck it up again anyhow! Makes
me sick, I tell you straight! When I think what one
could do with the money I've spent to load that ship
out there, I could—I could kick the emperor's arse!
But it's orders, I suppose, and I took an oath back in
the good old days when an oath meant something,
and . . . The worst thing about this trip, you know,
the very worst, is that when I get back I'm not going
to have a chance to plead my case. And that isn't fair!"

Finding his tongue at last, the host said, "Why
should you need to?"

"Because things are terrible everywhere in the
empire! I said so already, didn't I? To feed the greedy
court—and I don't just mean feed in the literal
sense—they've debased the money they gave me! I
got to Egypt only to find that because imperial
coinage mostly doesn't contain an honest quantity of
gold or silver anymore, they won't accept it except at
a discount! And you've no idea what damage that has
done to our creditworthiness . . . Jupiter Tonans!
I'm talking like a merchant myself now! But what it
boils down to is that I'm going home without a decent
load. This wine is all right, even though I had to buy it
in Alexandria and pay extra to cover the cost of
transport. The food isn't bad, though those Egyptians
don't seem to have learned as much about preserving
as you'd expect, given the way they used to pickle
their kings and nobles—but that's merchant-type
stuff, and any African grain ship might carry the same.

"No, what's wrecked the trip for me is the fact that I couldn't afford even one Nubian gladiator! Those lazy Egyptians haven't mounted a slaving expedition to Nubia in years—haven't even traded any in! If you go looking for blacks, all you can find on offer is kids, locally bred and most of them mongrels! Don't you think that's disgusting?"

He held out his empty cup again.

His host ruminated awhile, and eventually said, "You'd be interested in acquiring a black man? I mean, a full-blooded one?"

"Hah!" Cornax exclaimed. "I can't say someone like that would be worth his weight in gold, but if a lanista didn't buy him there are a thousand bored rich wives in Rome who'd snatch him quick as lightning, the ones whose husbands are too preoccupied with business or politics to look after them properly! You know what I mean!"

Disregarding the last sentence, the other went on, "Did you know there's a Nubian on Oragalia? Big, strong, and indisputably—uh—male?"

"What?" Cornax almost choked on his latest swig of wine. "How did someone like that turn up here of all places?"

"Presumably he's a runaway slave. Very likely he jumped overboard from a passing ship. At all events, last spring he was found living off the land, or in other words stealing from those who work to provide us with food. But he was on the south cape, where most of the time nobody goes—there's no land worth cultivating. And . . ."

He hesitated, eyeing the idol in the corner. Tense, Cornax urged him to continue.

"Well . . . Ah!" He was obviously searching for

the right words, but found them at last. "Well, there are some foolish ideas that the common folk adhere to, of a sort your honor is no doubt familiar with, and some of them relate to that particular part of the island, where in fact that statue of mine came from . . . Don't you admire it?"

"No!"—curtly. "Come to the point!"

"It's very old, I believe . . . I'm sorry. Anyhow, in the event the Nubian was left alone for a month or more. There was much talk of organizing an expedition to go after him, but—well, it shames me to say so, but an awful lot of our people, despite their braggartly words, turned out to be cowards when it came to the crunch."

Cornax tipped back his crude chair. (Oh for a decent couch like what one found at Rome! . . .) He said, "So you have a wild black man running around. Very well. The wildest man in the world couldn't stand up against a squad of my legionaries, so we'll collect him and take him to Rome with us. Use a net, probably. No trouble."

The other ventured, "As a matter of fact, sir, he isn't exactly wild. Not anymore, that is."

"In that case, what's the problem? Why hasn't one of your lot already recaptured this fellow and put him to useful work? It's legal, if he actually is a runaway slave—in fact, it's your civic duty. Why didn't you take on the job yourself, come to that? It looks as though you could do with some extra help around the place!"

"That's—uh—that's a long story!"

"I have nothing else to occupy my time until my ship is reprovisioned." Cornax leaned back further yet and crossed his legs. "You may recount it!"

"Well—uh! . . ."

"Get on with it, man!"

"Oh, since you insist . . ." And little by little the tale emerged, shorn of such embarrassing details as the speaker's complicity in the kidnapping of Anastasia's uncle and cousins, but full of allusions to the island's folklore. The latter were sufficiently commonplace for Cornax to get the drift of them.

The first report of the wild man had come from a boy taking goats to pasture. He could add up well enough to keep track of his beasts, and one day the count was short. Later, raw and bloody bones were found. Shortly after, a beekeeper discovered that his hives had been robbed of the first of the summer's honey. In the normal course of events, herdsmen and beekeepers were the only people to visit the southern cape of Oragalia, where the land was so poor as not even to have attracted the interest of the Roman who had had the aqueduct built, although in bad weather fisherfolk were glad to put ashore there.

Later the culprit was seen by daylight: tall and thin, blacker than the sun could have burned him, and apparently not just naked but devoid of tools, let alone weapons. However, as had already been indicated, although the islanders talked at length about tracking down and catching him, they proved unenthusiastic when it came to converting brave words into action. They seemed on the verge of deciding to put up with his predations, as though with a force of nature like gales and storms, when a certain woman cried them down and said she would achieve what they dared not.

They would have been overjoyed to see her fail.

"Why?" demanded Cornax, who for all the wine he had drunk was still alert enough to follow.

"Well—ah—that's another story! Suffice it to say that this woman had made herself unpopular. Perhaps she saw in this venture a means of worming her way back into people's respect, if not liking."

"And did she?"

"Not exactly."

"Man, make yourself clear!"—in a parade-ground voice.

Swallowing hard: "She made herself feared."

"Without much difficulty, I imagine. Judging not just by my limited experience of your particular island, but an extensive acquaintance with Greeks like you all over the mainland, Asia Minor and Egypt, I'd expect people of your stamp to scare pretty easily!" Cornax was rather enjoying this baiting of his host. "What exactly did this woman *do*?"

"She—uh—she tamed the wild man. Not only that: she gave herself to him, even though . . ."

"Jealousy! Jealousy!" Cornax crowed. "I see it now! You wanted her for yourself!"

The other stiffened. "That has nothing to do with it!"

"What does, then?"—with a positive guffaw.

"She went out to him farded and girdled like a whore, who had never yielded to any of our men! And next day she showed him to the folk, holding her hand as meek as—as anything!"

Cornax became abruptly sober.

"There's a story I heard when I was on garrison duty on the Persian frontier. It concerned a giant created by the gods to overthrow a king, and—"

"Right! Right! The king tricked the gods and sent a harlot in all her finery to seduce him—"

"And they became the fastest friends!" Cornax

jumped to his feet. "Oh, if I could take such a man to the emperor, with proof of the story, and the woman along with him! . . ."

"Excuse me, sir, but I was under the impression that it was the black man that interested you, not the woman!"

"Oh, go hire an Egyptian surgeon and ask him to sew your head back on," Cornax answered crossly. "I don't want her for myself! But surely it cannot totally have escaped the attention of you and yours that the emperors nowadays routinely consider themselves as gods! Here's a myth come to life, precisely what any emperor will pay a fortune for, and you wouldn't even have mentioned it if I hadn't pressed you! May Jupiter Tonans visit all the days of your life with thunder and lightning—well-aimed lightning!"

Swaying drunkenly, he yelled at his escort, dozing beside the entrance.

"Believe it or not, they've got an Enkidu here!"

"You don't say, sir!" one of the men answered cheekily. "What's that when it's at home, if I may make so bold?"

"Fool! It's not a what, it's a who!"

A surge of acidity rose in the back of Cornax's throat. For a moment he feared he was about to throw up in the presence of inferiors. Recovering, he went on:

"Just for that, Charon-fodder, you can head back to the ship and turn out the entire squad! At the double!"

Each and every time that Anastasia returned to the cave where she had found refuge—which was neither hers, nor her man's, nor anybody's, but a gift of

Mother Earth, who had reared up in fury (so it was said) in the not too distant past—she had to repeat, as though it were the first time over again, the actions that had led her to make a home here. The paradox obsessed her: she had tamed what everybody else dismissed as a wild beast, although it walked, and after a fashion it could talk, and in the other respects she had learned about was entirely human . . . and still, whenever she returned from the town, she wheedled, and lured, and cajoled . . .

She had been thinking "it." She canceled the concept violently. "It" was the pronoun her language applied to animals, or a child not yet of an age to reason. The lover she had chosen, strange and dreadful though his mien might be, was neither. *He* had proved it by his amazing tenderness and the gratitude which sometimes made him moisten her breast with tears.

As for the tumult *he* had created in her body . . .

For the first time she entered their den without setting down food beforehand, to tempt and reassure him.

Darker than shadows, he emerged from shadows and caught her in his arms, and took her swiftly in the way she most enjoyed—and then again.

Not until afterward was she able to utter the warning that she wished to convey. Then, slowly and with many misunderstandings, she explained that right now, right here on the island, were more of the people who had made him a slave.

She could smell the rage that rose in him.

But it was overcome by the realization that, thanks to her warning, he had a chance to hide. Moreover, surprisingly, he grasped the import of the ceremony, taught by Phoebe, which she next proceeded to perform. In the town there were not a few who claimed he had been allured by nothing more than her body, as a beast would follow its she in heat. That, though, could not be true, for unlike most of the island's menfolk he had waited for her invitation instead of jumping at her like a billy goat in rut. The Romans talked a lot, so she had heard, about "civilization"—essentially, the good manners that permitted many people to live together—but, given the Romans she had met, and the one who had kidnaped her uncle and cousins whom she hoped never to meet, or she would surely kill him, she was satisfied that this person whom everybody else called wild and dangerous was gentler and kinder than a thousand Romans added together.

Now, therefore, she produced the herbs she had gathered on her way back from town and put them to use. Squatting on his haunches, he watched with interest, and perhaps more than a little comprehension.

The task complete, she leaned back against the rocks. "In spite of all," she said, "they will come after us."

He grinned at her, as much as to say, "Let them be fool enough to try!"

And took her hand, leading her away from the cave—certainly the first place the Romans would head for—to lie out on the bare ground like a fox or a bird.

Wrapping her cloak tightly around her against the chill of evening, Anastasia lay down in the spot he chose for her. She felt apprehensive despite her precautions. The baby was kicking vigorously today, and she foresaw how eventually it would punish her with its feet, whenever she set it to her nipple, for the crime of expelling it from the warm safe womb into the harshness of the outer world.

That, though, was the story of human existence, and above all of this child's parents'. She had undergone much suffering; very likely life had been still crueler to its father, though she would not be sure how cruel until he learned enough words to tell her. He had not even boasted a pronounceable name until she bestowed on him the one that sprang first to mind: *the wellborn man.* It suited his noble bearing, despite the scars on his wrists and ankles which indicated that he had endured ropes and chains. Neither manacles nor fetters had closed around his soul . . .

"And our baby will have a freer life than either of us!" she promised the air as, reposing her confidence in the charm she had cast around the area—and still more in the strong arms of her Evgenos, who had acquired in his distant homeland the warrior's habit of not leaving anything to chance—she finally allowed herself to doze.

Tramping along the rough trail toward the south cape, with his crested helmet under his arm, Cornax started to feel distinctly unwell. He ascribed the fact to the badly cooked meal he had eaten, though a nagging suspicion remained that in fact too much Samian was to blame.

Controlling himself as best he could, he halted before reaching the highest point of the path, and shouted to the squad of men he had led hither.

"Right! Now you lot fan out, clear across the island!

Stay in sight of one another, though! Be prepared to run and help whichever of you spots the Nubian, and *don't* let him slip through the line!"

As they reluctantly complied, he cast a worried glance at the sky. He had thought they were setting out with plenty of daylight ahead of them, more than adequate to catch one unarmed man. Now, however, wintry clouds were drifting from the east, harbingering a sailable wind tonight or at latest by dawn. If by some ill chance they missed the Nubian this evening, would he be justified in staying another day when they were already so badly behind schedule?

And then a sudden horrifying thought struck him. *Was* there in fact a Nubian?

The more he reflected on the yarn which had been spun him, the more improbable it seemed. To start with, how about the idea that a slave could have arrived here after jumping overboard from a passing ship? If he were strong and healthy enough to reach the shore, he'd be valuable enough for his master to chase after him; if he were underfed and sickly, not worth pursuing, then he wouldn't be up to swimming any considerable distance.

Suppose the story were a complete fabrication, a subtle way for his host to get his own back after all the insults Cornax had lavished on Greeks in general and him in particular? Visions of the way the townsfolk might now be laughing at him filled the Roman's mind. He clapped his hand to his forehead. What a fool he'd been to swallow the tale at face value without questioning a few more islanders in search of corroboration!

He kept his misgivings to himself, but self-directed anger made his face as threatening as the sky.

There came a sudden shout. Excitedly he swung around, looking for its source. But all that had happened was that one of the men had managed to get himself stung by a belated bee, having trespassed too close to one of the wicker hives which dotted the stony ground.

"Keep quiet!" Cornax hissed.

The men around him exchanged glances, and eyebrows were raised. Come to think of it, there wasn't much point in silence when it wasn't yet dark . . .

Grumpily he trudged onward, wondering how the island could be so much wider than it appeared from the sea.

Beating the undergrowth, prodding with their spears, the soldiers discovered a starveling bitch, her hindquarters infested with botflies, nursing four blind pups, all of which they promptly killed; a stray goat with a broken foreleg, which they also killed—and cut up and shared, since it would make a tasty supper; a boy and girl aged about twelve, who had come this way to play games their parents would have disapproved of, and ran away in terror; a cache of oil jars, presumably stolen, three full and one half-full; the skull of a donkey; and a great many other miscellaneous items.

But there was no sign of a Nubian, or even of the woman alleged to have taken up with him.

They regrouped on the crest of the ridge overlooking the south bay. By now it was almost full dark.

"There's supposed to be a cave under here—go and check it," Cornax ordered wearily, indicating the two men nearest him. Then, as they hesitated: "Afraid he'll ambush you? Jupiter Tonans! All right—six of you go!"

"There's nobody here!" came the report a minute later.

Cornax sighed. Before they regained the ship it would be full dark, and tramping across such rough ground by night was a sure recipe for bruises and sprained ankles. Particularly if what you were looking for didn't exist!

He reached a decision. He would confront the man who had sent him on this fool's errand, and find out once for all whether there was any truth in his story. If not—oh, if not! . . .

"Very well," he muttered in disgruntled tones. "Back to the port. But you'll have to wait for me a moment."

Saying which, he hastily made shift to conceal himself behind the thickest of the nearby bushes.

Anastasia was awakened by the sound of soft and uncontrollable laughter. She started up in alarm. But the dark form that approached her out of darkness was Evgenos.

"Have they gone?" she whispered.

Raising her to her feet, leading her back to the cave, he explained haltingly, with the aid of many gestures hard to make out in the dimness, what it was he found so funny.

He had outwitted the Romans at every turn. The spot where he had told her to hide was already behind the soldiers when they spread out to search. Having found no trace of their quarry, they had stormed away to the town again, unaware that Evgenos was following them as inconspicuously as a stalking fox.

On arrival, their officer set about interrogating everybody he met concerning the alleged Nubian. But the islanders were either so afraid of Anastasia's revenge if they betrayed him, or so eager to see the backs of the Romans, they one and all denied any knowledge of such a person.

Whereupon, in a towering rage, the officer ordered his soldiers to whip the man who had deceived him until he fell fainting in a pool of his own blood, and furthermore to rape his wife and son, sack his house and make off with everything of any value, including his slaves. Since he was so cordially hated, nobody made a move to intervene.

Clasping her hands in wonder, Anastasia muttered a prayer of gratitude. Then she thanked her amazing lover in a more direct fashion.

Later, as they lay close for the sake of warmth, she murmured, "Naruhiko. Of course: Naruhiko!"

"Hm? What did you say? Was it someone's name?"

"Oh, Gene! You know perfectly well it was—and who I mean!"

"Ah . . ." He stifled a yawn. "I was half asleep, I'm afraid. What about the guy, anyway?"

"He was like a Roman in his way, wasn't he?"

"Stacy, honey, neither of us ever met him. So what makes you say that?"

"Oh!"—with a horizontal shrug. "Driven by the same forces: I guess that's what I'm getting at. He devoted his life to a search for constant excitement, you might say, spiced with a dash of glory now and then. Along came his chance to undergo a unique experience, and if all went well he could rely on adulation for the rest of his life."

"What became of him, then?"

"The place he went to was a world at war—not a cold impersonal war, but a nonstop succession of raiding expeditions, sieges laid and lifted, victories in single combat, the raw material for laudatory ballads which for a while would be on everybody's lips. Snatches of song celebrating his exploits followed him down the streets of whatever city he wandered to; countless women offered themselves, or their daughters; those whom he had defended against their enemies sought to reward him with silk robes, rare foods, the choicest tea and wine.

"For all of which he cared not a whit. The only gift he ever accepted was a sword.

"He felt himself incapable of love—which was one of the reasons he sought violent sensations, as a substitute—but if he did love anything, it was the company of his own kind, in drill before battle, in solemn ceremonies afterward, albeit at the funerals of the fallen. To him the discipline of an army surpassed all forms of art, and the code of honor of its officers was a prize beyond all earthly treasure. There was never any end, in this world he came to, of comradeship or glory . . . So he thought."

"Yet there were flaws in what he took for paradise?" Gene rose on one elbow and gazed at her, almost invisible in the nighttime blackness of the cave.

Stacy gave a sober nod.

"To be a paradise for everyone who desired the same from life as he did, it was necessary that the tide of battle turn. Later, he looked back with longing to the last day when it was his name the minstrels sought a rhyme for—his feats of arms which were recounted round the campfire—his command which led the van and broke the enemy. There were just as many valiant achievements to make ballads on, just as many deeds of skill and daring, just as many victories as ever . . . and, inevitably, just as many defeats.

"So it became his turn to leave the field weary and alone and beg at the doors of peasant shacks where people hated him and all his kind. Ultimately he was reduced to selling his armor, piece by piece, in order to buy food, and when nothing else was left except his clothes, his shoes, and that single gift he had accepted, his fine sword, he sat cross-legged beneath a tree whose leaves dripped rain, and faced the truth."

9

THE EXHIBIT

is the broken head of an idol.
It symbolizes an attempt to control the universe

THE MONTH

is December

THE NAME

is Olga

EVERY MORNING, ON A SHELF OF ROCK NEAR THE cave, there appeared such offerings as the folk of the island could afford. They scarcely amounted to wealth: a bunch of onions, a few figs or olives, a salted fish, a cake of coarse meal mixed with water and charred rather than baked over an open fire, smeared with honey if the god of the weather had been kind.

But there was always something. Even the advent of the black stranger had interrupted the succession of gifts for only a single day.

Most of them were brought by children compelled by their parents to scurry through the predawn dark in order to discharge a duty they did not yet understand. Now and then, though, maybe half a dozen times a year, a more substantial donation was silently placed on the ledge under cover of night: a well-glazed pot, a knife, a fleece or goat hide, even— but this was very rare—a minted coin.

And such objects presaged a request for the services of the pythoness who dwelt in the cave.

Typically, next morning there would be someone waiting at the same spot, not a child, but an adult, or at least a youth or girl: wanting to know, perhaps, whether to accept a parent's dictates concerning a planned marriage; or which of a group of brothers destined to share a minuscule inheritance would fare best if he quit the island to seek his fortune; or how to recant an ill-considered oath without incurring the vengeance of the god whose name had been invoked. This person would have waited since midnight in fear and trembling, for it was no light matter to consult an oracle. Indeed, occasionally the supplicant's courage failed, and he or she only reappeared days after delivering the necessary fee.

Once the seeress had had a name like anybody else's. She had been born here, and grown up, and though her mother had died bearing her a good few relatives survived, so they and sundry others remembered what she had been called in youth. But since she entered into her full powers few people, apart from those who now verged on senility, had referred to her in any other manner than as "One who has lived before." On the rare occasions when the islanders encountered her, gathering herbs on the ridge that spined Oragalia, or jetsam along its rocky beaches, they reacted in one of two ways: either they beat a prompt retreat, as befitted those who knew about the sacred mysteries but were not party to them, or they ran to her and begged a favorable charm.

To the latter she was sometimes affable, sometimes

tolerant, sometimes insulting. News of her response would spread within hours, and later, in the isolated farmsteads, there would be arguments lasting past sundown about her current mood and what actions of their own might account for it. Every place in the world, it was known, must be under the aegis of some tutelary deity or other, and they and theirs were constantly at loggerheads. They must be, for earth, sea and sky were full of forces surpassing the comprehension of puny humans, and the nearest anyone could come to accounting for them was to invoke the image of a quarrelsome family. It was advisable to keep on the right side of anyone with insight into such arcane matters.

Moreover, few communities—and that included all the neighboring islands—enjoyed the luxury of their own seeress. There were oracles aplenty on the mainland, but they were a long and dangerous journey distant. In any case, what attention could those alien gods be expected to pay to somewhere this remote and insignificant? Let all rejoice in their good fortune, then, inasmuch as they benefited from one woman's contact with the divine.

So great, indeed, was the confidence the folk reposed in her that they now neglected many antique shrines, and had let former ceremonies fall into disuse, to the vast annoyance of the royal family, for they provided the hereditary priests or priestesses of the cults concerned.

The king himself had ruled harshly in the past, thereby earning the detestation of his subjects. Now, though, he was old and ill, and unwilling to waste his failing strength in a fruitless struggle against one chosen of the gods. However, seeking what they regarded as their rightful share of the people's offerings, his kinfolk tried repeatedly to persuade her to take the king's last unwed son in marriage—a beardless boy!—or at least accept one of his daughters as a pupil and companion.

All such proposals she rejected with fine scorn, and the folk came reluctantly to believe she was resolved to die a virgin.

Unpredictable as ever, last spring she had proved them wrong.

Where he had come from, the black stranger, no one knew. None of the fisherfolk had reported finding so much as the wreckage of a raft after the storm that presaged his advent. Some claimed he was not human, but conjured up by magic arts from the infernal realm of Hephaistos the lame smith. At all events, one morning of a sudden he was there: starvation-gaunt, yet exceptionally tall, black as midnight and naked apart from a spotted animal hide wrapped around his loins, a figure of indescribable menace.

The children bringing the pythoness's daily offering encountered him in twilight, dropped their burdens and fled in terror. When they reached home, at first their parents accused them of telling lies, but when they themselves ventured near, nervous, after sunrise, there he was squatting on a rocky outcrop, gnawing twigs off a tree bough—for food, they thought at first, mistaking him for an animal.

Then they realized he was stripping the branch to use it as a club, like Heracles, and ran away as swiftly as the children.

By noon almost the entire population of Oragalia had assembled to stare at the dark-skinned apparition. Some, urged on by the king's eldest son who craved action because he was growing weary of waiting to enter into his birthright, were brandishing weapons and declaring that this monster should be put to death at once. Others, however, were not so sure it would prove vulnerable to swords and spears.

While they were still arguing, the pythoness appeared bearing a bowl of broth. To their amazement, she was even more naked than the black man, for she wore nothing but a charm on a thong around her neck—though her nudity was already a powerful magic.

Approaching the stranger, who desisted from his task and watched her warily, she set the dish just out of reach at a spot where the breeze would blow the savory aroma toward him. Then she stepped back and waited.

Suspicious, but leaving his club behind, he was lured toward the bait. Having dipped and sucked his finger, he approved the taste, and after gulping down the broth greedily scooped up the remaining scraps.

The pythoness held out her hand for the bowl. He relinquished it and said something in a language no one—not even she, apparently—could understand. She smiled, and offered her other hand to take his. Uncertain, he shied away and snatched up his club. But she stood her ground, and only moments later he made up his mind to go with her. Together they disappeared in the direction of the cave, leaving the king's son and his cronies to disperse discomfited.

Next morning, when the offerings were brought—

not by children for once, but by burly armed men—
he was there, watching from a nearby crag, leaning on
his club. And so it had been every day since. The only
difference was that now the islanders had grown
almost proud of having such a wonder in their midst,
and even the children called greetings to him, which
he had learned to answer, in a gruff tone but
comprehensibly. Also, since the weather had turned
cool, he had donned a coarse woolen cloak.

The change in the pythoness herself was far greater,
for now she went with child.

At first the islanders had refused to believe it, being
so convinced she was committed to perpetual chastity.
Then those who maintained that the black stranger
was not human, but forged by the smith of the gods,
pointed out that this would mean a line of succession
was to be established. No doubt such a child would be
possessed of powers even more amazing than its
mother's. Fortune would smile on Oragalia forever!

Apart—as usual—from the king's kinsmen, the
populace were delighted to fall in with this reasoning.
After much debate, they even decided to act in
accordance with it.

Today dawn broke on a figure waiting at the usual
spot on the hill above the bay, but there had been no
special offering, nor was there one now. The common
sort of food had been sent, only it had been brought
by an uncommon carrier: an old woman, nearly
toothless, her skin like wrinkled leather, but her
hands still strong and her eyes still keen. Shivering
perhaps less from the chill than at the sight of the
black man, whom few had dared approach so closely,

she remained where she was when he emerged to collect the food.

He challenged her—or greeted her; it was hard to know which—and she replied in a steady voice, but he did not have enough words to grasp what she meant. Satisfied, however, that she posed no sort of threat, he returned to the cave.

A while passed. The sun broached the horizon.

Then, moving slowly, for her time could be at most a fortnight away and her belly was so big that the child might well be born early, the pythoness left her cave and mounted the steep path which snaked past it, upward to the ridge, down to the beach. She spoke in irritable tones. The crone explained her presence. On being curtly told to go away, she glanced nervously at the black man, but remained where she was.

Sensing, if not following, the meaning of the exchange, the man pantomimed picking her up and throwing her over the cliff. The pythoness seemed to consider the idea, but eventually signed no, and let herself be led back to the cave. Lying on a heap of skins and fleeces, she managed to convey despite many false starts and misunderstandings the fact that the woman was a skilled midwife. The folk had decided that those with such knowledge must keep guard here by day and night from now until the birth-time, for fear of any delay in being sent for when labor started. The life of a pythoness's child was too precious to be risked.

Abruptly catching on, he grinned, his teeth amazingly white in his dark face. Seizing a piece of meal cake, he dipped it in oil and returned to the hillside.

The old woman cringed when he advanced on her,

but he took her hand gently and folded her fingers around the cake, then pointed at his mouth. For a moment she seemed to think she was supposed to feed him. Perhaps imagining this was some sort of sacred ritual, she made to do so, but he burst into a rich deep laugh and indicated more clearly that the food was for her. Surprised, but willing enough, she mumbled it with a word of thanks. Later, he brought her water in one of the pythoness's fine glazed pots, before setting out to check the fishing lines he had laid along the beach.

At sundown the watch changed. A younger and stronger woman arrived and sent the crone hobbling homeward. Before departure the latter handed over a ball of twine and a knife, its blade honed to flashing keenness, which she had hitherto kept concealed under her cloak. The black man thought at first it might be meant for self-defense, as though even at her age the old woman feared assault from this ferocious-looking stranger. Hah! In the case of the new arrival, on the other hand . . .

Seeing him stare at the knife, however, she demonstrated its use, pantomiming the emergence of something between her legs, then gesturing with the string and sawing at the air. Light dawned, and he shook his head vigorously. In the land he hailed from, women brought similar instruments to attend a birth, though generally of bone or polished stone. There, too, they would have reacted in just the same way as this one did when he held out his hand and mutely requested a chance to inspect the symbols engraved on the haft. She thrust the knife behind her instantly.

Well, it was women's magic anyhow. He turned away into the gathering dark.

"Olga!" he said suddenly.

It was very late. Stacy was only drowsing, though, not fully asleep; the child was kicking at her furiously as though eager to be born. So far, however, she had not warned him of the onset of labor pains. According to her best estimates, they ought not to begin for several days.

Shifting in search of a comfortable position, failing to find one, she snapped, "I'm not called Olga! Who's Olga?"

Recently she had reverted to her former abrupt changes of mood. Wanting to calm her, he laid a soothing hand on her cheek, and withdrew it instantly, sitting up.

"You're sweating, but it's chill tonight!"

"Don't worry—" she began, but he was already reaching for a rag to dip in water and wring out. Having laid it across her forehead, he rested on one elbow, gazing down at her dim outline.

"That's nice," she sighed. "Thank you . . . Gene, I'm sorry. I didn't mean to snap. Of course I know which Olga you mean. Tell me her story. Maybe it'll help to send me to sleep."

"That's a backhanded compliment if ever I heard one," he muttered. But he lay down again, cradling her head against his shoulder, and stared at the invisible roof of rock as he marshaled his words. At length:

"Maybe it was her background . . . though how can one ever be sure what's outside influence and what's innate? At all events she grew disillusioned with intellect and reason. She spent her life searching for experiences which would transcend reality, and when she was offered the chance to do so in the literal sense, she seized it with avidity."

"What was the proper world for Olga, then?"

"Not in any real sense a world. At best a place. A place where rationality no longer ruled. The frame of logic was strained there, coming apart as it were to offer glimpses of something else beyond, insusceptible to reason.

"First of all she noticed that certain of the events which happened to her resisted explanation. The people she had come among were happy to accept them, seeking no underlying cause, and after a little she realized that this was precisely what she'd always claimed to want.

"Habit, however, was too strong. A meeting she desired took place when it should have been impossible, the other person being much too far away. An object she chanced across, but could not find again, seemed to have been of a color not belonging to the spectrum. A phrase she overheard in someone else's conversation rang with subtle meaning, but she could neither grasp that meaning nor repeat the words. Strive as she would to enjoy these experiences, she found them dreadfully disquieting.

"Growing desperate, she was ultimately driven to the conclusion that the fault must be in herself, and set about rectifying it, by laying herself open to more and ever more extreme stimuli. At first she made the error of rushing to locations where events she regarded as improbable had been reported; after a while, however, she realized they would never be repeated and hence one spot was as good as any other. It was pointless to go anywhere, or do anything, when one did not understand the logic beyond logic. By definition, though, it could not possibly be understood.

"Yet everything seemed possible where she was, at least in the sense that impossible things were happening every day.

"This insight offered a degree of comfort. She made the most of it. Forcing herself to concentrate, she set about demolishing within her mind the assumptions she had regarded as commonsensical throughout her life. In this way she hoped to attune herself better to this new reality—if reality it could be called."

Gene paused. Stirring at his side, eyes closed, Stacy prompted, "Did she succeed?"

"You can't say 'she' about her anymore. There was success, that's all. The identity which had been Olga's melted like a snowflake falling in the ocean. At the last—the very last—moment, she realized that even if she did achieve her goal, there would no longer be an Olga to rejoice."

"It was too late."

"For her, it was too late before she started out."

10

THE EXHIBIT

is a world ateem with life.
It revolves around a variable star

THE MONTH

is December

THE NAME

is Anastasia

IN PITCH DARKNESS STACY STIRRED UNEASILY, AWARE of a dull cramp in her abdomen. At first, muzzily, she took it for a touch of colic; she felt bloated and flatulent, as though she had eaten something which disagreed with her.

She strove to remain asleep in spite of her discomfort, for she had been having an elaborate and fascinating dream. Indeed, she was still partly lost in it, for her mind was aswarm with images and sensations, all of them astonishingly vivid. Normally she recalled her dreams as mainly visual, with perhaps a phrase or two of conversation, or a snatch of something that might, for the right person, have turned into a fragment of a poem. Never before had she experienced any which extended to involve the totality of herself, both mental and physical. Heat and cold were there, bodily posture, sounds and smells, hunger and fullness, happiness and despair, the feel of clothing on her body, wind on her cheek, sunshine and rain . . .

Oh, this dream was extraordinary, and seemed to have no limits. It was as complex and detailed as reality, and moreover it was populated with a countless horde of people. She could literally see and hear them with her eyes tight shut—or even open, for in the utter blackness it made no difference. She felt as though she were drifting past them, carried by an invisible river of air, so light she could not sense her weight on her heels. As she drew near to each individual or group, she could hear talking, sometimes shouting, sometimes laughing, now and then discussions in low tones concerning confidential matters which she could not make out, no matter how hard she strained her ears. But that was of small account, for at her approach they invariably broke off their conversation and turned to gaze at her, their expressions varying from hostility to puzzlement. She looked in vain for sympathy, and could not work out why she should be seeking it.

Was it in fact at her that they were staring . . . or someone at her back? She was aware of a presence behind her, but she could not turn around, no matter how she tried.

The effort of recollection itself was making her more and more wakeful. Still she fought to retain the dream's images and sequence of events, determined to impress them on her memory despite renewed pangs.

To some extent she succeeded. Clear as life, she saw an old woman in a greasy cloak of undyed wool hunched on a low flat rock, her hands concealed but clutching objects of enormous purport . . .

(Images of separation and binding; they presaged a monstrous tearing apart, as though the cosmos itself were to be riven into shards.)

And a line of grim-faced men, their arms and legs bare but their bodies encased by harness of tough leather with studs and plates of bronze; they carried spears, and oblong shields hung at their backs on leather thongs . . .

(Images of division and compulsion; they had the power to snatch husband from wife, mother from child, and ordain that they belong henceforth to other people.)

And a noisy mob of soldiers, clad in rusty mail and with daggers at their sides, who had not yet drawn the latter and were brawling more in fun than in earnest . . .

(Images of terror and superstition; they had been told throughout their lives that their cause was just, and in spite of all the wickedness it had brought into the world they were prepared to entertain no alternative.)

And men and women traveling in carriages from stately home to stately home, their clothes a triumph of the tailor's skill, scorning beggars as they held out talon hands and showed off oozing sores . . .

(Images of isolation and antipathy; they literally could not accept the poor as people like themselves, and felt more pity for a foundered horse than for a human.)

And a gang of rowdy merrymakers shouting and drinking around a table and cursing the attendants for their slowness to obey orders in a foreign language . . .

(Images of debauchery and shamefaced lust; they wanted to deny quotidian reality, break loose into a temporary otherworld where they might rule unhampered, yet kept encountering obstacles they could not disregard.)

And an army drilling in impeccable order, every movement as precise as a machine's, rehearsing to unleash a hell of horror on their fellow creatures, but disguising it behind the trappings of an artificial art . . .

(Images of exultation and destruction; they held themselves superior to nature herself, but knew no way to prove it save by humiliating and debasing other people.)

And the crew of a vessel tossing in mid-ocean, cursing salt meat, weevily flour and water foul enough to make them vomit even without aid from the waves, reviling the captain who had lured them on a voyage to far continents . . .

(Images of misery and greed; they had signed on as much because their lives at home had grown unbearable as because they truly hoped for riches on return.)

And a shifting crowd of persons garbed in silk and satin and brocade, standing on a quayside among bales and bundles and barrels; beyond them, a hedgehog's back of spiky masts that rocked and tilted like a dancing forest . . .

(Images of bargaining and distribution; they could coax and wheedle the ignorant into parting with what they needed most and sell it on to those who already had too much.)

And an empty beach, newly created by a rise in the level of the sea, which until a generation ago had been twice her height above the water, overlooked by a cave whose entrance was framed by concrete pillars once as formal as a propylaeum, now tilted and off-square as though they had been earthquake-struck—

The darkness was full of a roaring noise. For a second she thought of it as the grinding of just such an earthquake, only infinitely worse: the sound of space-time being shattered and remade—a memory. Then, through her still-closed lids, she realized there was no more darkness. Boat had diverted what remained of her power into turning on her searchlights, making night into day, and the racket was the chattering of a helicopter coming in to land.

Abruptly she realized who and where she was, and whose presence at her back had been during her dream. Also she registered that her pain was arriving in rhythmical waves and there was wetness between her legs. Opening her eyes in terror, she found that the cave had been invaded by men and women peeling off coveralls to reveal green sterile clothing. Alongside them marched machines on legs, better than wheels for such rough going. Some of them, fitted with their own lights, carried TV cameras. Humming softly, they settled around her like vultures beside a corpse-to-be, and the people closed on her like ghouls.

Oh, this was *wrong*! Here, now, should be a time of solitude, when the magic and mysterious process of making a new life reached its fulfillment! What business did strangers have to intervene? Or anybody? (She had almost loved someone; she must learn to love her child—children . . .)

She begged for mercy and surcease; they gave her none.

They had dealt with Gene first, in case he interfered with what they planned. Awakened by the row, he had started to his feet and rushed to the cave entrance. A silent machine like a chrome-plated stick figure awaited him. It was impeccably programmed. The back of his head sank into a resilient pad and a band closed around his neck; his arms, his torso, his legs were matched from behind by clasping metal limbs with joints in precisely the right places to let him move provided he did so very slowly. At the least hint of an attempt to break loose, they locked solid.

Also there was the sting of a diadermic on the inside of his left elbow, on feeling which he screamed.

Because at that instant dreadful memories stormed in.

He was cocooned into rigidity and weightless (she also). His face was covered by a mask (like hers). Food and water belonged to his past and maybe future (and hers). Taped to the crook of his elbow (and hers) there was a pipe warranted to deliver sufficient nourishment into his veins (and hers). It was to keep him (her too) alive for an hour before, a week after—and who could say how long between?

Would there be time?

There was nothing to do except report his subjective perceptions. Everything else was taken care of by computers. He was very frightened, and said so once or twice—but they would know that already, because they were monitoring his bodily condition. Minutes ticked away. He could see a clock, but no other instruments—what use would they have been? At least the designers had been thoughtful enough to site a window where he could look out of it, and a couple of times he began to count the stars it made visible. But the stabilization was imperfect, and new ones drifted into view while others vanished, so he kept on losing track.

Around him amazing energies assembled. Eventually his nerves started to sing, as though the fabric of the space he occupied were being warped.

Well, that was true.

He began to feel a sort of separation from himself, his thoughts becoming dreamlike and random. The sensation was not unpleasant, though the frustration he experienced when he tried to describe it was. In fact it became worse than just unpleasant. It became infuriating. He wanted more than anything to flee back into his own past and cancel the decision which had led him to this utter loneliness on a path that others had dared, only to return insane or dead.

As the clock closed on its zero, he found his voice one final time.

"I must be out of my mind!" he cried.

And was, for the universe shattered.

Tore apart.

Dissolved.

Ceased.

There were not, never had been, could never be, words to describe the experience.

Except perhaps it felt a bit like being a billion people at once . . . and all of them dead.

Yet he was here: in his body (he sensed the pounding of his heart); breathing without a mask; able to see and hear and feel and doubtless speak, once he could summon up the energy to do so, which had been filched from him by the injection in his elbow. Right now talking didn't seem all that important.

Curious, he gazed around as though he had never seen this place before—and in a sense he hadn't, for not even at midsummer noonday had there been such brilliant light in here. Over the months he and Stacy had brought ashore many of the facilities from Boat, but some were too heavy, some called for power they could not provide, and some she was forbidden to part with by her original programming, so the home they had created was by no means luxurious. Indeed, it now disgusted him, for there was a heap of rubbish by the entrance as foul as a medieval midden (did I pass that every day and disregard it?), and the bed they had shared was—

Best that he could not see it past the clustering people and machines. But it was all being recorded, of course: every last minutest detail . . .

"We couldn't let you go on with your playacting any longer," said a stern voice nearby. Gene turned his head as quickly as the machine that held him in its clutch permitted, and saw that the speaker was a woman with short brown hair, thin enough to be mistaken for a boy, though with betraying lines of age once one looked closely at the skin below her jaw. She went on, "Her waters have broken. She must have been in an incredibly deep sleep, practically a coma. Otherwise the first stage of labor would have roused her, and that must have set in two hours ago . . . Oh, stop looking at me like a stranger! I'm Dr. Catherine Hoy—as you're perfectly aware!"

Hoy—boy . . .

"No, you're not," Gene said wearily. "You're Bony, the cabin boy, and you helped to row a boat ashore from that Venetian galley. Where's the captain?"

He tried to turn his head further, but the movement was too hasty for the suspicious machine, and it locked up. Dispirited, he let himself slump against it, whereupon—with due and automatic caution—it relented.

By that time, something more important had claimed his attention. Closing his eyes briefly, he sought words.

"If you say you're called Hoy, and you're a doctor, I guess I have to take your word for it even though I think you're someone else. Doctor or no doctor, though, what I want to know is what you're doing to Stacy. And why!"

"You know why!" came the curt response.

"Simply because she's going to do a perfectly natural thing, and have a baby?"

"Under the most primitive and insanitary conditions!" Hoy flared. "Man, what possessed you to play along so with one another's fantasies? We held back until the last possible minute, but when the birth pangs started—"

He raised his eyes to meet hers, a motion the machine permitted, and for a long moment she was abashed at the intensity of his reply.

"There have been no fantasies, Dr. Hoy. There have been realities."

He was beginning to understand what had happened to him (to them). A sense of intersection filled his mind: yesterday as real as tomorrow and neither any different from today. How to make Hoy recognize the truth whose force had suddenly pervaded his very bones? Suppose he were to say outright, "It's true the universe is solid! So where you sent us must be somewhere else . . . yet we did come back!" Would that plain statement penetrate her world of preconceptions? No, she would not grasp the implications. Could anybody, without having gone where he had been, without treading the long path back through time? It would be like trying to share a dream.

At the same instant, anyhow, Hoy was distracted. A clear faint voice spoke from midair, inquiring how things were progressing, and she snapped a response to the effect: "As well as can be expected!" There followed a number of technical questions, and a request to couple up some item of equipment via a satellite connection to a main computer on a distant continent. This was attended to.

Gene took advantage of the respite to gather his wits. When Hoy turned back to him, he was able to say, "You didn't have to go to all this trouble. The local midwives have been taking turns to stand guard near the cave so they could be called on as soon as labor started . . . Oh, *now* what's wrong?"

She was staring at him with mingled pity and dismay.

"I didn't understand till this very moment how deep your delusions were running," she whispered.

"Gene—oh, Gene! How long ago did those midwives promise to stand by?"

"Why, yesterday!" he answered in bewilderment.

"You poor crazy fool! I'm sorry, but that's what you are! This island of Oragalia has been depopulated ever since the water level rose. Your 'yesterday,' as near as we can guess from eavesdropping on you and Stacy while you talked with your imaginary friends, must have been about *three thousand years ago!*"

Had there not been a trace of sympathy in the serious faces which confronted him, at that point Gene might have broken down. Instead, fighting to digest the knowledge that was now invading his mind like floodwaters after a downpour too great for any ordinary channel, he folded his fingers into his palms until he felt the pain of his rough neglected nails, and clung to something Stacy had said when they were talking about—whom? It didn't matter. All that counted was what she had said, about being crazy: "My guess is that it must feel normal."

And he had known and accepted from the beginning that one of the countless risks he was running was insanity.

After a long dead pause punctuated only by mutterings from those attending Stacy, Gene said with such calmness as cost him all his self-control, "We searched Boat from stem to stern. We threw away all the monitors and microphones because we were so desperate for privacy. But you cheated us. You had our home bugged all the time."

"I think normality is creeping back," said Hoy with satisfaction, then caught herself and adopted a gentler tone. "Yes, Gene. We were prepared to respect your wish to be alone. We all agreed—me and Professor Shaw, Professor Yiu and Dr. Ngota, everyone—that we'd kept you far too long in a laboratory situation, and it was time we had a chance to observe your reactions in a setting nearer to everyday life. It was your coldness, you see, the remoteness that you both exhibited. Neither of you could be called insane in any clinical sense. You behaved normally enough; you slept, you got up on time, you bathed and dressed yourselves and turned up for meals and underwent our tests and answered our endless questions, yet gradually we became aware that your attention was elsewhere, and so was hers. You were acting like programmed robots, not like human beings anymore. Something was wrong, and so we let you go, daring to hope you'd make a full recovery.

"Instead, you became more and more lost in a maze of dreams. And then, when Stacy became pregnant . . . Well, without us what would your today have been?"

"Real."

"What?" She blinked at him.

"Real!" Gene repeated. "To me, now, all of this is artificial—hideously so! I want to be beside her, hold her hand, watch while the baby comes, do what a father must and should to help her . . . You won't permit that, though. Will you?"

"She has the best possible care," Hoy countered stiffly. She gestured in the direction of the bed. "Right over there you can see the finest obstetrician we could find, the best anaesthesiologist, a team of top experts flown here at short notice just to help her! And you, of course," she appended hastily.

"I think you're here to kill her," Gene said with terrible directness.

"And I think"—in a soothing tone—"you're over-wrought. It would be best if you had a chance to relax."

She reached out with her fingertips and rapped a code on the machine that held him. There was another prick, this time inside his other elbow.

The world vanished instantly—and not just *the* world, but all the worlds. More worlds than there were any means to count.

They had usurped control of Stacy's body, too, disposing her in what official wisdom decreed to be a proper posture. In the no-longer darkness of the cave, she was being kept as still as the convulsions passing through her would permit. She had been intending to let nature take its course. Nature was not to be allowed to. As helpless as when she had been hurled into impossibility, her physical self remained passive while her mind sought ways of—escape? No, continuance. The ancient realities held: birth, nourishment, learning, making, breeding, teaching, dying . . .

Suddenly frightened, she groped with closed eyes for a familiar hand, whispering, "Gene? Gene!"

But what she touched was smooth plastic overlying something solid, which vibrated but did not respond. No one seemed to notice that she'd stirred.

A snowflake dissolving in the ocean . . .

"Gene . . ." she murmured in a failing voice, and knew that her lost mind now had no haven to return to.

11

THE EXHIBIT

can walk and talk, can suffer and dream.
It keeps asking how and to what purpose

THE MONTH

is December

THE NAME

is (in both senses) Gene

I CAN'T FIND A WAY BACK!"

He was moaning. He could not hear the words, but he recognized them from the shape his tongue and lips imposed on air, and he knew what he meant whether or not anybody else did.

"Gene!"

Not his voice. A firm, commanding one, which he ought to recognize—only something far more important occupied his mind. He said, "There's no way—but there must be!"

"Gene, don't pretend you're talking in your sleep! We know you're awake!"

Oh yes, indeed, he was. His brain was crackling with insight like a thunderhead sparking lightning from peak to peak—against a gray-black ground of misery.

"Gene!"

So why would this intrusive bastard not listen to

what he was saying? In sudden rage he reared up and shouted.

"THE UNIVERSE IS SOLID, DAMN YOU—SOLID!"

But as a shout, it was feeble, and his rearing up was frustrated by the fact that he lay on a couch of such resilience, his elbows sank into it, deep, deep.

He had, though, forgotten until now that his eyes were shut.

Opening them, he saw bright scudding grayish clouds. It was high noon—insofar as noon could be high on this, the shortest day of the year. He was no longer in the cave. He was on the afterdeck of a smart modern ship, much larger than Boat and far better equipped, a prime example of the generation of seagoing vessels called into being by the loss of so much land after the thawing of the ice caps. And he was afraid of what might be in store for him.

Did they plan to peel his mind apart like an onion, layer by layer, with a skill born of centuries of practice? It had happened to him before—how long ago? It could at most have been one year, yet it felt far further in the past than the three thousand Hoy had mentioned.

But if they tried that again, all the knowledge he had garnered on his trip beyond the limits of infinity might well be lost forever. He would no longer preserve the difference between himself and them. He had to stop it happening, and he had no faintest notion how to do so.

This bitter conclusion made him take proper stock of his surroundings. It was not an open deck he lay on. He, and those near him, were enclosed by a perfectly transparent bubble: invisible, yet nonetheless a cage. He reached out a hand, and there it was, as though the air had solidified. One side of the bubble was formed by the white flank of the ship's bridge, and the sole door set in that was like the entry to an armor-plated bunker. He wasted no time on looking for cameras and microphones and the hidden sensors that would trap and analyze his very skin secretions. He took it for granted they were there. Once more he was not a human being, but a specimen. All he could do was cling with might and main to his own self . . .

But who was he? What was he, who remembered being the jock who ran away with an heiress—the shipwrecked fisherman who claimed the hand of an island's most marriageable virgin—the slave who swam through stormy seas to liberty and love? Who was the man who had traversed impossibility and come home whole?

He didn't know.

But perhaps (suspicion grew at the edge of consciousness) he knew who was the mistress that had claimed him.

A shiver crawled down his spine, although he was not cold. There was something awe-inspiring in that thought.

"Gene, look at me, will you?" the same voice said.

Remembering that for a while he had not even been able to turn his head, and relishing this petty degree of freedom, he complied, and focused on the man who was leaning over him. The face wasn't right—No, more exactly, the garb wasn't. He wore a peaked cap and a white jersey, and he should have sported a brown velvet slouch hat and a stained doublet . . . The captain of the Venetian galley! Of course! And Hoy equaled boy, and where was Scarface?

This sensation was abominably unpleasant, as though he were a set of badly meshing gears.

"I read recognition in your eyes," the man said softly. Gene summoned concentration and made shift to answer.

"Yes, you're the captain," he answered in a dull tone. "I didn't register your name when you visited us. Why didn't you come straight out and tell us who you were?"

"When was that?" the man countered, glancing sidelong. Hoy appeared next to him. Still no sign of Scarface . . .

"Why, when you brought us all that strange food . . ." But the memory grew dream-elusive as he spoke. "Anyway, this is the wrong ship. You had oarsmen, and your sail was furled for lack of wind. And you talked incredible nonsense!"

"For example?"

"Oh, you tried to tell us . . ." Gene squeezed his eyes shut with effort, but it was useless. Concepts, phrases, images that sprang to mind vanished instantly, lost to him behind as dense a barrier as the one that walled the universe. He found himself saying over and over, "It's solid! You've got to understand me—got to!"

The man raised his eyebrows, once more glancing at his companion Hoy, and now they were at last joined by the one Gene still thought of as Scarface . . . but he differed most from recollection.

Clad in a quilted cotton jacket, he was thickset and square-faced, and his cheek was as remembered scarred, but it was pitted with the traces not of a wound but of disease. At any rate, though, he was sallow and his eyes were shaded by the epicanthic fold.

He said, "Make sure he realizes who he's talking to."

"I know only too well," Gene muttered. "You're Professor Yiu—hah! You're yiu! Of course! Sorry about that. Bad joke. It's just that I need to find something funny in the world, or I'll go mad . . . And"—forcing himself into a sitting position despite the reluctance of his too-soft couch, so he could look directly at the captain—"I'm *shaw* about you as well: Benedict Shaw."

"So you finally accepted that," the other murmured. He had a clear and level gaze. He had never actually worn a brown velvet hat. "What else do you recall?"

"Infinitely more than you, if you live to be a million."

"That isn't quite what I wanted to know," Shaw returned patiently. "You recall my name. But do you remember—ah—what post I hold?"

"I held a sharpened one. Used it to dig that bad salty ground."

"We'll come to you in a moment. We're talking about me."

Abruptly further obstinacy seemed fruitless. Gene let himself slump back on the couch.

"You're the chief psychologist of Project Go."

"What's that?"

"It's all to do with ships."

"What kind of ships? Ships like this? Ships like Boat? Look, there she is yonder." He pointed.

Reflexively Gene turned his head. Indeed, she rode at anchor off the western cape of the beach where he and Stacy had—had . . . That, though, was beyond him to define.

She was somewhat battered after nine months at anchor off this rocky shore, but not greatly harmed. Also she was no longer alone. She had been joined by half a score of other vessels.

"I'm waiting for an answer," Shaw prompted gently.

"Oh, damn you . . ." Gene passed a hand across his forehead. "Why do you have to pester me like this?"

"Because you accepted it might be necessary. Now we say it is."

That was logic he could not dispute. He murmured, "If there is a hell, perhaps it consists in living up to all one's promises."

"What?"—from Hoy and Yiu together, while Shaw knit his brows in search of meaning.

"Oh, never mind. Of course I know what sort of ships!" (The stark metal hulls; the scentless stench of artificial air; the vacancy beyond; the rawness of the force they summoned from the sun . . . His body was pouring sweat in torrents.) "Just as I know who I am and Stacy was!"

"Then say it, man! Say it aloud!"

"Ships to exceed the speed of light! And we your sole successful guinea pigs!"

Hoy uttered a yell of delight and flung her arms around both Shaw and Yiu. Shaw, though, pushed her brusquely aside.

"You said: 'who Stacy was'—" he had begun, when a harsh voice interrupted from the air. The sound was directionalized, and Gene could not hear clearly, but the other three instantly lost interest in him and Shaw began to issue a series of brisk orders. A few moments later, there was an indistinct commotion on the beach. Shortly the helicopter's blades blurred and it rose swiftly from the sand and headed back this way.

A premonition clutched Gene's heart. With immense effort he forced himself over the side of the couch and rose, swaying. Nobody made any attempt to stop him. Anyhow, it was too late to do more than he had done already. Maybe three thousand—maybe a million years too late . . .

"The baby!" he exclaimed. "What's wrong with it?"

"Nothing's wrong with the baby," Shaw said curtly. "By the way"—in a more placatory tone—"it's a girl."

"Then what—?"

"We don't know! We'll have to wait!"

Deep within himself Gene found some resource of calm, and though he realized it might be due to drugs was grateful for it. Without such help, he would have gone berserk. Aching, he stared as the helicopter touched down the other side of the invisible barrier. Its door was flung open and Stacy was lifted out on a stretcher.

On seeing her clear, he felt terror no chemicals could disguise.

For her face was covered by an oxygen mask, and even as the stretcher was lowered to the deck a technician scrambled after, striving to keep in position on her naked chest a shiny chromed electrode.

"I did say 'was,' didn't I?" he whispered.

Shaw nodded, and his face turned paper white.

After the stretcher, they unloaded something else from the helicopter: an oblong box with a soft but tough transparent lid, an incubator, with two nurses in attendance and many tubes and instruments attached to it.

"Let me out!" Gene cried. "I must go to her!"

Shaw, having listened to the air again, laid a hand on his arm.

"There's nothing you can do, Gene. I'm desperately sorry. It seems there's nothing anyone can do."

"What?"—not wanting to understand.

"Her heart will not respond. They don't know why."

Gene's hands fell to his sides in a posture of uttermost defeat. Turning away, he muttered, "I do. I said to Hoy: you came to kill her. And you have."

"We came to help her!" Hoy exclaimed.

"Help her? *Help* her? She didn't need your help! She was doing exactly what was right to save herself! If only you'd let *me* tend her—she'd taught me well . . . Oh, you idiots!" Clarity was returning to his thoughts by giant strides as his subconscious found ways to turn insight into words. Had they not drugged him—

No, it would have been too late in either case.

As well as rage, a hint of resignation showed in his voice when he went on.

"Haven't your computers figured it out yet? No? Then what use are they?" He took a pace toward them, and they flinched back against the unseen wall.

"There's Stacy dead, and you wouldn't even let me hold her hand while she was dying, and you don't know why it happened anyhow! I do! She sent you a message by the only means you left her, and you ignored it because you thought you knew it all—didn't you?"

"We never claimed—" Shaw began. Gene cut him short.

"The message that she's sent you is her death *in birth*! She opted to die! Opted to, d'you hear me? Because she knew she could never find her way back to any world that we call real unless she bore our child when it was due—three thousand years in the past! And you, you *fools*, dragged her back to the here and now without a by-your-leave!

"Now you've stranded me on my own, without her, without anybody, loster and lonelier than any refugee that ever was! Oh, I've found *my* way home—she's made me whole by leaving me to spell out a message you lot are too thick to interpret, and I know that because I'm mourning her! I can feel again! I'm no longer just responding like a robot, and I only wish I could hate you as much as you deserve!" Glaring, he clenched his fists.

"I want to hate you for all the reasons in the universe! I don't care how much time, how much effort, how many people you've spent on trying to find a way to reach the stars! You've had your chance, and for all I ought to care you and everybody else might find your own way to hell! You've sent me there, and now you've slammed the door on my escape! Because I dare not hate you—not after the sacrifice she's made for all your sakes! I'd be betraying her!"

Abruptly there were tears streaming down his cheeks. He turned to the side of the ship's bridge and leaned his forehead against its smooth white surface.

After a while he began to beat his fists on the painted metal, moaning what sounded like a blend of all the names by which his mistress had been known to him.

This too was recorded by the dutiful machines.

12

THE EXHIBIT

is small and weak and ignorant and helpless . . . but alive.
It's you, and me, and everyone, as we once were

THE MONTH

is any month

THE NAME

is its mother's, and your mother's, and mine too

"**S**O HERE'S ANOTHER CHILD WHO'LL ONLY EVER know her real mother."

Gene's words hung heavy on the air. It was warm, but in his heart there was eternal winter.

Shaw responded after a dreadful interval, leaden as the silence of the grave. His face was gray and lined, as though he had aged a lifetime in a single day.

"I wish I could believe you're mouthing nonsense. But I'm terribly afraid you're talking more sense than I can grasp, even if it is wrapped up in riddles."

An hour remained before sunset, but for the sake of the inevitable concealed cameras multiple lamps shed their brightness in the ship's resplendent cabin, where he, Hoy and Yiu sat opposite Gene on deep comfortable couches. At least they were treating him like a human being again, instead of trapping him in a barless cage for computerized interrogation, which was what he had been most afraid of.

Because they were shamed by Stacy's death? Because he had guessed right when they were wrong, even though they believed him to be crazy? Who was to say what was sane when nothing like it had ever happened before?

At least Shaw was making a valiant attempt.

"You have a beautiful daughter," Hoy ventured. She seemed to be very far from understanding. "The obstetrician assures us she's in perfect health."

Their eyes turned to the incubator on its shiny metal trolley. Gene was staring down at the baby's wrinkled features through its transparent hood. He had insisted on placing it where he could see her clearly. The others, at worse angles, saw only patches of reflected light.

He had also insisted on certain objects being brought from the cave where, magpie-fashion, he had accumulated them over the past nine months: a brochure from a last-century travel agency, its colorful photographs smudged by seawater; a handful of empty shell cases from a World War II gun; a Victorian preserving jar, its glass lid chipped and its rubber sealing ring long perished, but its wire closure intact despite corrosion; a weathered icon recovered from the half-drowned church; the hilt of a sword, its blade shortened to a stump; several shards of decorated pottery which he had painstakingly assembled until their common form appeared, hinting at a jar for wine or oil; a broken tile bearing the graffito SEP:IUL:CORN:LEG . . . but the rest was lost; and a fragment of a preclassical idol, half a head, showing one ear, part of the chin, and hair in braided lines as neat as well-plowed furrows. All these were landmarks in what had happened to him and Stacy.

The survivor said eventually, "Have you worked out yet why it had to be her and me, not any of the others?"

The others exchanged glances. Hoy said at length, "We're evaluating various hypotheses."

"You can take your hypotheses and—!" But Gene's reflex fury died before he completed the sentence. Wearily he corrected himself.

"After what I said just now, I hoped you would have. Your minds seem to work so slowly, though . . . Okay, I'll have to do it the long way.

"You weren't responsible for choosing us, I admit. But it should have been you who figured out why Stacy and I proved more resilient than the rest. I know why we were allowed to volunteer, of course. Everything had gone wrong when they used smart people like trained scientists. So maybe it would succeed with someone ignorant, who could be relied on to react instead of reasoning."

"Gene!" Hoy was half out of her seat. "That's scarcely a fair description of either of you!"

"Yeah, it applies better to Shanti, right? I recall we talked about her one night. But you must have all that down in your computer records." He appended a sour grin.

The other three were tense as skyhook wire, aware that now Gene alone might hold the key to the universe, desperate to find out what he could teach them to help in planning future expeditions, but at a loss to know what they could safely say without provoking a renewal of his fugue.

Making a desperate effort, Yiu/Scarface ventured, "If you've figured it out, we'd be glad to hear your views. Can you express them for us?"

Express . . .

The word was /pregnant/with meaning. Gene said reflectively, "Can I convey the truth to you? I doubt it! If you could be so unforgivably stupid as to kill Stacy, you must be too thickheaded to catch on! In fact you are! You didn't hear what I said about my—our—daughter!"

But even after silent consultation of the computers which were monitoring everything that transpired in the cabin, the others continued to exchange baffled glances. Gene lost patience.

"Oh, get me a drink and a bite to eat, and I'll explain . . . Has *she* been fed?" he added, indicating the cot.

"Yes, exactly as if Stacy—" Hoy bit her lip.

"I get it," Gene said with heavy irony. "You've programmed a computer to synthesize colostrum. As though any machine, any creation of our own . . . Never mind. That can wait."

He leaned back and cross his legs, staring through the portholes toward the silhouette of the island which had almost the shape of the sphinx, poser of the riddle he had unforeseeably learned how to answer. After a while he began to weep again, soundlessly.

Later on, though, setting aside an empty glass and a plate with nothing on it but crumbs, he spoke calmly enough—indeed, in a meditative tone, aware he was putting everything he said on record, aware it would be analyzed and dissected by a thousand strangers. But he was used to that.

"I kept saying: 'The universe is solid.' Did you at least latch on to what I meant by that?"

The others nodded uncertainly. This exceeded the boundary of their own specialisms, but they had perforce been brought in contact with the concept.

Shaw said at last, "I think we did, but we'd rather you explained it to us."

"What's to explain? Even at the lowest level beyond the ordinary quark, every time an event occurs which can have more than a single outcome, all the outcomes do in fact take place. This makes the cosmos solid, in the sense that there is no more room inside it for anything else."

He hesitated, tilting his head to one side as though striving to hear a voice at the limit of audibility, and added in a half-surprised tone, "Hmm! Maybe that accounts for the way I used to claim that thanks to my ancestors my subconscious pictured the universe as a continent which could be trekked across . . . until I realized that Stacy's view was precisely the reverse, and she'd survived at least as well as I had, so one of us had to be wrong. In the upshot, of course, we both were, so—

"Never mind that, though. It's for later, when I can spare time to mourn her properly. Right now what matters is that this explains why, for so long, people were content to accept it was impossible to exceed the speed of light.

"Not that most of us imagined it would ever become necessary to try and do so. Here we were, on this small but comfortable planet, cheerfully abusing her hospitality as though her resources were inexhaustible, fighting wars, squandering our children's patrimony as though she belonged to just one generation, smugly convinced the rest of the universe was much too far away to worry about—except perhaps the sun, and so long as that rose every morning! . . .

"And then—!" Gene uttered a harsh laugh. "You know, I'm beginning to wonder whether something out there decided to teach us better!"

Suddenly afraid he might have disturbed the baby, he leaned toward the cot, but she was sleeping peacefully, and he resumed.

"At all events, that sun we'd taken for granted for so long turned out to be a variable star, didn't it?

"Oh, the experts who educated me and Stacy before our respective trips had worked it all out afterward: how minimal the fluctuation, how long the periodicity, how difficult to detect at a distance of even a few light-years . . . Nonetheless, it was enough to change the world.

"Not just by melting so much ice that the ocean level rose and half the people on the planet died, either as a direct result or because of the wars we fought to claim the remaining land. More importantly, it scared the rich and powerful among us in a way they'd never been scared before.

"Space travel had been a toy for the wealthy countries, hadn't it? They put up their communications satellites, they dreamed of establishing a High Frontier, they spent a little time and money on exploring the Moon, Venus and Mars—but always in the expectation of a payoff, if not in cash then in prestige. Survival was very far from people's minds in those dead days. Oh, some planned against the risk of war, but only a handful thought about keeping human stock alive were some universal catastrophe to overtake the Earth. And then, all of a sudden, our so-trustworthy sun—! Hence desperation; hence meteor mining and crewed trips to the other planets, which served only to confirm they could never be rendered fit for habitation. Hence, in the upshot, Project Go."

Shaw leaned forward. "It's hard for me to say this, but I think I must. Our first volunteers all died or went out of their minds. Would it be true to say that you and Stacy too became what's generally regarded as insane—if less extremely so—but that you had to because there was no alternative?"

Gene looked at him with fresh respect. He said, "Now it's your turn to spell something out. I can tell by their expressions that neither Hoy nor Yiu have caught on yet."

The others confirmed with nods. Dismayed, Shaw leaned back, gazing into nowhere.

"I'll do my best, but how to frame it in words? . . . Ah! There was a question no one thought to ask."

"I hear you," Gene encouraged.

"Well—what becomes of 'I' when it's doing something deemed to be impossible?"

Silence fell, broken finally when Yiu exhaled.

"Oh, yes. *Oh*, yes! But why you two?"

"Because, like her," Gene said patiently, and rested his hand on the incubator that enclosed his daughter, "we only knew one true parent."

"How are you going to call the baby?" Hoy demanded with a flash of insight. "After her mother?"

"I thought about that, since they tell me Anastasia

means 'resurrection.' But—no. After *my* mother, and Stacy's."

"But you're an orphan!" Yiu was shaking his head in confusion. "So was she! How will you name the baby, then?"

"After my mother! I just told you! And yours, and everyone's! Now you've remembered about orphans, surely you must be able to figure out why only she and I came back healthy and partway sane. If not, there's little hope for humankind!"

He surveyed them, his expression challenging. Realizing that Yiu, confused, was about to call on the omnipresent aid of computers again, he checked him with a glare.

"Heaven's name, man! Have you so far forgotten how to reason for yourself? Then maybe we should abandon the universe to machines, like Suleyman!"

"You talked about him and all the others, didn't you?" Hoy probed, struck by sudden recollection.

"Yes, of course. Why?"

She put a hand to her forehead. "I almost see it but it keeps eluding me . . . Your mother, and ours, and hers too—Wait a second. You're arguing that you survived *because* you're an orphan, and so is Stacy?"

"Was"—in a tone like the grinding of icebergs.

"Was," she accepted. "Sorry. But is my guess right?"

"I still don't know what it is."

She bit her lip. "All right, I'll do my best . . . Even though so many of the human race had been left parentless after the oceans rose, from the beginning we of Project Go selected people who had known a stable childhood. There must have been an unspoken assumption that they'd be better able to withstand

John Brunner

the new experience. But you and Stacy came back in
far better shape than they did, even if you did
eventually decide to run and hide from us . . . Are
you claiming that that was our main mistake?"

"Of course." Gene spoke over his shoulder while
pouring himself another drink. "The worst mistake
you could have made. Who wants to leave behind, at
the probable cost of life or sanity, a parent who's been
kind and trustworthy? Not till you scraped the bottom
of the barrel—not till you'd met with so many failures
that any average person would decline—was Project
Go obliged to turn to folk like me and her. We neither
of us knew a mother apart from Earth herself."

"Your daughter's name, then?" Shaw demanded.
"Terra."
And, as one, they imagined he'd said *terror*.
But in a sense it would have been the same.

Later:
"You talked constantly of the—the ones who didn't
make it," Shaw muttered. "There's a hint of a pattern
in our records which I can't make out; none of us can,
and it's too subtle for even our best computers. I have
a dreadful suspicion that it will turn out to be as
obvious as the connection between orphanhood and
your survival, once you show us what it is . . . but
you'll have to."

"I say again: who wants to leave behind a loving
parent? And what motives are there to venture into
the unknown?"

"Oh! . . ."—from Shaw in a sort of sigh. "I got the
picture. Finally I got it. You reviewed those motives
one by one."

"If I'd only realized you didn't understand—" Gene

muttered. "But there's no help for that. We still can't turn back time, though I dare believe that some day . . . Ah, but that must take very long to learn. Probably none of the science we've invented yet will show us how. By then, Stacy and I will be forgotten; so will you."

He drained his glass and set it by.

"Yes, we experienced—we didn't plan or map, we simply underwent—the reasons that there are for leaving home. Call on your computers if you don't remember in what order. For me, it's all as clear as yesterday."

Though yesterday can be three thousand years ago . . . He felt a pang of dizziness. It passed. He waited for someone else to speak, recalling that he owed a duty to his species.

The air filled with a susurrus of sound not aimed at him. Hoy said, "Well, first you talked of Suleyman."

"Who went in search of certainty," Gene grunted. "It's not allowed—not even to machines."

"Ingrid, then!" Shaw snapped.

"Worship. And gods or goddesses that fail are spurned."

"Cedric was next," Hoy said, frowning. "Was his quest not also for certainty?"

"In some sense, yes, it was. But he sought it from his own convictions. No faith can possibly suffice. It's always undermined by ignorance."

"Oh, this is absurd!" Yiu burst out. "You never met these people, and we did! We recruited them, we trained them, we prepared them as completely as we knew how! What you're saying about them is based on—on guesswork!"

Gene gazed at him stonily. He said, "It stopped

being guesswork a long time ago—a thousand years at least. When we started to sense why we were cast adrift in time."

"You mean you were aware—?" Yiu began. Gene cut him short.

"Not until the very end. I said 'sense'! Do you have to turn every last gut feeling into words?"

"Let's finish the list," Shaw suggested placatorily, laying a hand on Yiu's arm. "Shanti?"

"Indolence! A life of ease!"

"We already mentioned her," Hoy said, biting her lip. "But who was next? . . ." She listened to the air. "Oh, of course: Giacomo."

"You talked about him the day we decided to risk visiting you in person," Shaw said. "We were worried about malnutrition. We'd kept Boat well stocked with provisions, but you seemed to be neglecting them in favor of what little you could grow or catch. Some of the food you forced down . . . Hmm! That's a point I'd like to clarify. So many of your—your *episodes* seemed to turn on food."

Gene stared at him in blank bewilderment. At length he said, "But there's no nourishment in space! It is this world that's always fed us: Mother Earth!"

"Yet our source of energy remains the sun!"

"Oh, yes: the Father, as it were, who got us in a womb of primal mud. But do you feel that to be true? Do we absorb raw energy, like plants—or Suleyman's machines?"

For a second Shaw's eyes locked with Gene's; then Hoy said, "I can't feel it, in the sense he means, and I doubt that anybody can. It's a question of intellectual acceptance . . . We were talking about Giacomo, weren't we?"

"Whose motive was perhaps the only noble one," Gene sighed, reaching for his glass.

"Was there not a noble element in all cases?" Yiu countered. "Is not self-sacrifice a noble thing?"

"Sometimes," Gene answered grayly, "it's due to nothing nobler than despair . . . But he was a true explorer, granted. You who knew him told us so. The lust for discovery is relatively pure, compared to some of what we've talked about."

"I . . ." Yiu shrugged and leaned back. "Okay, I accept that. Please go on." Cocking his head, he once more checked the data the computers were supplying. "Hedwig came next."

"Ah, yes. The missionary. That says it all."

"What?"

"Think about it." Gene leaned to confirm that the baby was still asleep. She was, though a discontented scowl was dawning on her face.

"But surely she was driven by a high ideal—"

Yiu broke off in confusion. Hoy and Shaw had laughed.

"This time at least," the former said, "I see what Gene is driving at. To dream of changing the whole universe in accordance with a set of local preconceptions! . . . Oh, it's ridiculous!"

"A missionary," Gene repeated with a solemn nod. "By definition: a person who does without intending it more harm than good."

"The verdict of history," Shaw sighed, deciding to copy him and take another drink. "Ingrid shared some of the same characteristics, of course. Now I come to think of it, I realize where you borrowed her story from."

"I don't get you," Gene said, blinking.

"That makes a change . . . Sri Lanka, if you want to know. Over two thousand years ago there was a king in the island who irrigated vast areas and made them flourish for everything except people. Before he decreed his reservoirs there were no mosquitoes. They came, they bred, and spread malaria. His kingdom died."

Gene uttered a soft chuckle. "Well, that proves what I'd started to suspect: no matter what far world we talked about, it was always Earth—always, because we know no other."

"Missionaries act as though they do," said Hoy in a somber tone. "Go on, Gene. You still haven't told us what you thought about Pedro."

"Poor fellow! With his plain and shameless greed!" Gene seemed to relax for the first time since this interrogation started. "What crueler fate than to set up as a merchant of unprecedented goods, only to find no market for them?"

Thoughtful, Hoy said, "So far you've talked of explorers and missionaries and merchants, but—"

Yiu interrupted, having once more had his memory refreshed with the aid of computers. "I want to hear your view of Naruhiko! He was next!"

"One more addition to the list of motives: conquest."

"But according to the story you and Stacy told—"

"He conquered nothing in the end? Oh, no! He did. He was obliged to."

"What?"

"Himself."

The trolley carrying the incubator was fitted with microphones to pick up any sound the child might make. They relayed a whimper, and Gene was prompt to drop to his knees beside it. But she was only stirring in her sleep, and after a moment he resumed his seat.

"That leaves Olga," Shaw said. "I can't see where she fits into the pattern you're outlining. Was she perhaps an exception to the rule?"

"There are no exceptions," Gene retorted. "The universe includes every possible event, and events include all our thoughts, because we're in it. I still can't be sure—probably I'll never know—whether I 'thought' in any sense while I was *out there*."

For a while they were overwhelmed by the totality of his outness. At length Shaw returned to his point.

"But, according to what you and Stacy said to one another, she was searching—"

"For something beyond the universe? Oh, indeed! But she was found insane, remember, when they caught and opened up the ship she'd flown in."

At this reference to the fate of so many pioneers, they all felt a pang of the chill which had pervaded Gene since he was told of Stacy's death, and had long ago eroded the mental armor loaned to him by drugs. None of them had been hurled past the barrier of lightspeed, but they had all flown space during the desperate quest for starflight; they had endured the burden of knowing, awake and asleep, that nothing protected them from death in vacuum save a flimsy metal hull, which any speed-massive particle from otherwhere might breach . . . Shaw said, "You found what she was after. You survived. And then you went—?"

"Back to our mother," Gene replied.

"I do believe I understand at last!"

"More than I do!" grumbled Hoy.

"Or I!"—from Yiu.

"Now listen!" Rounding on his companions, Shaw hammered fist into palm. "The ship they flew in—Stacy first, then Gene—it did exceed the speed of light, correct?"

"And was the first that we recovered in good enough order to be used again," said Hoy. "We all know that! So what?"

"So this! Gene has made it clear that he, his ego, his identity, his 'I,' was—was squeezed out of existence during the trip, and had to find a way home! And likewise Stacy's!" Shaw was almost babbling with the intensity of insight no computer could have offered.

"So far, so good," Gene said drunkenly. He had filled his glass yet again, in search of protection from full awareness of the loss of his beloved . . . yet in a sense she was still with him, and with everyone—Oh, paradox!

Shaw leapt to his feet, pointing to the objects Gene had had brought into the cabin.

"They *had* to run away from us! We interrogated them, didn't we, pestering them over and over for information they didn't yet know how to put into words? Remember their helpless bafflement when they replied to our questions and in their turn asked how come we didn't understand their answers? I thought, like everybody else, that they were mad to flee, because there was no place on Earth or off it where they could escape surveillance, but now I believe they were sane to choose this island for their refuge, because it forms a link with all our roots—a bare and stony nowhere-much, yet full of relics, a counterpart of this our planet, whose history is writ in rock formations!"

"But why?" Yiu demanded.

For a second Shaw glared at him. Gene interrupted, rising to his feet.

"It can't be helped. That's the way it is. Until this generation, all the voyagers who ever set forth—even the crews of the ships we sent to Mars and Venus and the moons of Jupiter—fell into the same plain categories as we were used to, the ones that Stacy and I discussed. Most were explorers eager for new knowledge; some looked for new worlds to conquer; some hoped for profit; some were simply bored or scared by ordinary life.

"But lacking patience as we do, the only way to reach another star, for us, is to take a route outside the universe. It can be done, and I'm the—living—proof . . .

"*Where, though, outside it, is there room for mind?*"

While they sought an answer to the unanswerable question Shaw had posed, Gene indicated each in turn of the relics he had had brought in.

"Because of this"—brochure—"Stacy and I were able to relive a past of luxury and relaxation, when there was no fear of what the sun might do except it gave you sunburn!

"Because of these"—the empty shell cases—"we were reminded of the way so many people fled from war, as refugees! When we found this"—preserving jar—"it made us think about planning for tomorrow, or next winter, or next year. And as for this"—he caught up the icon and held it before his chest like a

shield—"it forced us to repopulate an empty island!
You came, you saw us then, *and didn't understand*!"

He was panting with the violence of the truth he
struggled to impart. Shaw said in a thin voice, "That's
true, and I'm ashamed. Above all we failed to
understand that the people you were 'meeting' all the
time had once been real. I still don't have the faintest
notion how, but we checked back over what records
concerning this island had survived the Flood, and
name after name proved to correspond with what
we'd heard over the mikes in your cave: Hamilton,
Kreutzer, Osman, Cornax—Greek, German, British,
Turkish, Roman . . . There's no way you could have
learned from trivial relics like these"—a thump on the
table—"who they were and when they came to
Oragalia!"

"I could have told you how that came about if you'd
left us alone! . . ."

Gene laid the icon down and swallowed hard.
"Well, anyhow, you didn't, and your damned machines—! Forget it; it's too late. My lady's dead, and I
dare not cry for fear of waking Terra."

The ancient implications of the name made them sit
still and pay attention.

"By then we knew what path we had to take for
home: no path you choose, but one you let compel
you! With a force as irresistible as hunger, our
instincts guided us unquestioning along a road we
never dared imagine, like a wild animal on the spoor
of prey! Resist? As well resist a whirlwind! And all we
had for to guide us was this junk! Look at that"—the
sword hilt—"and think about the hatred and the
madness it implies! Consider the false convictions
that informed its wielder, sure of his faith!"

THE TIDES OF TIME

He was trembling worse than ever.

"And yet this madness is true knowledge, nonetheless! We found our way to this"—he touched the fragments of the broken jar—"and started to suspect the basic facts.

"What you prevented us from doing when you charged in with your pigheaded preconceptions and your steel machines . . . *was finishing our journey home.*"

"Are you implying"—this faintly from Hoy—"that we'd done the same, only worse, to the others?"

"Hooray!" Gene crowed—and was instantly concerned that he might have disturbed the baby, but she did no more than fidget at the noise.

"You mean the volunteers that survived might have—have come sane if we'd let them go on being crazy?" Yiu complained. "I don't follow that at all!"

"That's obvious," Gene sighed. "Try following me the rest of the way, though."

He laid his hand on the tile with the Latin inscription. At once Hoy said eagerly, "I get the association with conquest and taking over, but I miss the next bit."

"Good. It had nothing to do with that."

Baffled, she blinked at him, and he stamped his foot with rage.

"Just pay attention to my words! Open your mind and let the truth pour in! We'd finally worked our way to concepts of settlement and occupation—not conquest, but living somewhere else! Is that plain enough, or must I repeat it again, and again, and again?"

Under his glare Hoy shrank back, abashed. The

226

force of his fury and frustration seemed to make the atmosphere crackle, as with invisible lightning.

"Thank *you* at long last! There's one thing left!" He picked up and kissed the broken face of the idol.

"You've got to accept that we came to this planet as though we ourselves were colonists. Okay, we evolved here, but the moment we developed imagination we cut loose from the limits imposed on lesser animals. So we grew lonely—lost in time, as no other creatures on the Earth could be. We did our best to turn the living rock into something we could talk to like another person; we sought chance resemblances in wood and stone, and eventually carved idols. Here is one." He set it down again, and paced the cabin, both fists clenched.

"Oh, I see it so plainly, and I can't convey it! . . . Let me make one last attempt. I'll ask you all to think about *rejection*."

Shaw tensed. He said, "That's strange! It was a word the others used—all of them—and I just realized I never heard it from you before . . . or Stacy," he added, as though embarrassed at the mention of her name.

"You can't mean 'all,'" Gene corrected in a glacial tone. "Suleyman and Ingrid were recovered dead."

Shaw met his gaze. "We had the tapes," he murmured.

"Yes. Yes, of course. I'm sorry; please go on."

"About rejection? What rejection is there more complete than being forced outside the very universe?"

"Now finally," said Gene, "you've understood."

* * *

The sun set on the implications of his words. Eventually Yiu stirred and sighed. "You had already been rejected, though—and Stacy too. At last I see the import of your comment about your daughter. It isn't rational but it's a fact: the only rejection that's comparable is when a parent dies before or at your birth."

"Out there," said Gene, "that doesn't matter any longer. But the earth your mother and the sun your father—they are the ones to whom you must return, the prodigal."

"And beg to be forgiven?" whispered Hoy.

"Yes, indeed. And there remains one question you've not asked. I think you know what it is. I think you are afraid to put it to me."

He waited.

At last Shaw stirred, not looking at him. He said, "It could be this. Who were the people that populated your—your—?"

"Fantasies?" Gene offered wryly.

Shaw shook his head. "I have to accept that travel outside the universe makes nonsense of conventional divisions between what's real and what is not. It'll be years before we digest the implications of what you've told us. I'm asking about—" He had to swallow hard. "I'm asking about the people who seemed real to you in other ages. How could they correspond so perfectly with a past you never had the chance to research, whose traces since the Flood are so scarce and hard to find that none of our archeologists can contradict your view of it? You even invented sailors from the Venetian period to disguise us when we were right there in front of you!"

"I don't know how to answer." Gene frowned, deep

furrows developing between his eyes. "I can only"—
with a sidelong glance at Yiu—"hazard a guess. This
island has been a crossroads of the world. I think they
may have been . . . well, forebears."

"Literally?" Hoy stabbed. "And physically?"

He didn't look at her. "Past a certain point there's
no way that can matter. All our predecessors are also
our ancestors."

"Three thousand years is far too short a time for
that!"

"Of course it is." Gene bestowed a skeletal smile on
her. "But it's as near, it seems, as natural law permits."

"You mean you couldn't find your way back to a
closer time?"

"Ah! You're finally accepting what I say as true!"

She bit her lip, hands writhing in her lap, and said,
"You and Stacy were each outside the universe for the
equivalent of—"

"Don't guess; calculate. Or get your computers to
do it for you. Our voyages were carefully controlled:
we flew in the same ship for the same time, though
not together, and by then the tolerances were down to
fractions of a microsecond. Yet because we've built so
fragile a bridge of intellection between the primal
state and ships that can traverse the impossible, it
took Stacy and me *three thousand years of detour* via
the past before we could reconnect with the continuum of human experience. Or would have done,
had Stacy been allowed to bear our child."

"Why?" Hoy erupted to her feet. "What's so
marvelous about giving birth? Millions of babies are
born every year!"

"Because"—he met her gaze levelly—"it's a miracle
every time it happens. It's the only way we have to

communicate between the past and the future. It lifts us out of time to raise a child that will survive us. And, like it or not, the deepest levels of the subconscious mind accept that as a greater truth than any other."

"But now we can travel faster than light—"

"Another door has opened to the future: yes! Something in us has overcome the limitations of the physical universe, something you and I and all of us possess. Mind? Reason? Intelligence? We have plenty of words for it, but no faintest notion which is aptest. All we can say is that we can do this thing, and when we do it, whatever makes it possible is forced outside all of space and all of time, and has to find a route back to reality for which there are and very likely can be neither maps nor charts. Explaining why may take a million years."

He concluded in a slow, grave tone, each word bearing its full burden of unprecedented meaning. Under the impact she sank back in her seat, her face pale.

"In that case is there any hope? Shall we in our time be able to send colonists to other stars?"

"Oh, very possibly. But I doubt whether those who survive the trip will long remain human in any sense you or I would recognize. After all, they'll have to learn a road back to reality along the worldline of a planet which is not our own. What to do about that, of course, is up to you to figure out, not me. But there's something comforting about it nonetheless—isn't there?"

Unexpectedly, Yiu gave a smile. "It matches the traditions of those teachers who have always said: we are not as bounded as the universe."

"That something in us can exceed it?"

"Yes!"

"Well, I'm a proof of that, I guess. But as to what you or I or any of us can do with the first objective evidence for immortality, I've no idea. Right now—" Gene drained his glass and glanced toward the porthole.

"Right now it's dark. I must bury my dead."

"What?" Hoy stood before him, rocking back and forth on her heels. "You just said we are immortal after all, and now you're talking about a burial—!"

"What I went through, Stacy went through too. It hasn't stopped her body being dead, has it? Nor has it changed our nature!"

Of a sudden, she folded her hands and turned away, sobbing. Retaining his composure, he laid his hand consolingly on her shoulder and spoke to her and Shaw both.

"Take care of the child. I'll come back at dawn. Find me a spade and carry Stacy to the beach."

"Oh, Gene, surely—!"

The intervention came from Yiu, whom he silenced with a scowl. "My journey isn't over! One thing remains. I must accept she's past recall, and so must you. With luck, tomorrow I'll be as sane as anyone, more so than most. I've been on a longer journey than any other of my kind, and it must end as every lifetime journey ends: with the acceptance of death, and a new birth. *Do as I say!*"

"But," protested Yiu, "you just said you're the proof of our immortality!"

"As usual, you didn't get my point, but I was thinking of *her*," countered Gene in a voice as cold as tombstones. He peeled back the cover of the incubator and touched his daughter's cheek, featherlightly. It was too much. She woke up fretting and began to wail. A nurse who had been eavesdropping rushed in and scolded him as she caught the baby up to comfort her.

"Gilgamesh," murmured Shaw.

"What did you say?" Gene rounded on him. "Was it a name? I seem to remember it, but . . ."

The other hoisted himself to his feet. "Yes, the Roman that you fantasized about—or maybe met. He mentioned Gilgamesh and his boon companion Enkidu. It's the oldest story in the world. It tells of the king who lost his best friend when the gods sent a plague against his city, so he set out in search of the herb of immortality. Such was his love for Enkidu that when he found it he would not use it himself. But he fell asleep beside a pool, and it was stolen from him by a water snake. Then, when he came home, he was so changed that at first his own people failed to recognize him.

"But when he died, they wrote his epitaph, and I recall it word for word."

Solemnly, in the manner of one performing a ritual, he closed his eyes and recited: "'He went a long journey, was weary, worn-out with labor, and, returning, engraved on a stone the whole story.'"

There was a pause. Even the baby, as though she understood, fell silent in the nurse's arms.

"Give him the spade," said Shaw at last. "It's time he had the chance to be human again."

Epilogue

Hoy and Shaw laid Stacy on the beach, wrapped in a shroud—of natural fiber, which would rot. Gene had insisted.

He waited in the gathering dark until they went away. Then he whirled his spade at the full stretch of his arm and tossed it up to the headland he had selected for her burial, thinking how much higher would have been his cast before the oceans rose.

Gathering her body to him, he struggled up the steep and rocky path. He was not altogether surprised when near the top he sensed a presence at his back. He laid her down at last beside the spot that he had chosen, and looked around.

There were so many of them that he could not count. All were a little faint, a little indistinct, yet now and then he caught a detail as the clouds above parted and revealed the moon: there the glinting of a watch's crystal; there a military cap badge; there a rusty iron helm . . .

Also there were other signs: a waft of incense, the echo of a chant.

But mostly and above all there were silent folk in drab plain clothing, whose very bodies knit the land together into flesh and bone.

Not questioning, he plied his spade and dug a pit. He'd chosen well: this was the deepest patch of earth above the rock. His muscles rejoiced in the resistance of it.

But they wearied, and when it came time to lay the body in its grave he was glad of the help of those who carried it. He recognized them: Milo Hamilton, and Leutnant Kreutzer; Osman Effendi, and the captain of the galley; the honorable knight, and the shipmaster from Africa; the angry officer who hated emperors, even the old woman who had sat day-long in case her skill was needed, who hobbled up and spoke a charm as earth was tossed to cover Stacy.

After that, for a while, he was blinded by tears.

Much later, when dawn was lightening the sky, he found himself among a crowd around a fire, which he had no memory of having lit. They were in solemn mood until the sun pierced the clouds; then they passed wine, making no offer to share it with him. As day broke, they doused and scattered the embers and revealed baked meat—just meat and nothing more. They divided it and gave a piece to all.

To all, save him.

Then, with looks of infinite pity, each provided for a journey into somewhere else, they took their leave.

He sat awhile on a cold flat rock, aching but unable to move, until full daylight overtook him. At last he leveled the earth and made his slow way down the path again, back to the shore.

His long, long trip was over. Now he could make clear to those who planned to follow how best they might prepare themselves to take the road around the universe, yet never lose touch with the continuum which was all the life and all the lives of humankind.

Waiting on the beach, he found he still knew how to smile.

ABOUT THE AUTHOR

John Brunner was born in England in 1934 and educated at Cheltenham College. He sold his first novel in 1951 and has been publishing sf steadily since then. His books have won him international acclaim from both mainstream and genre audiences. His most famous novel, the classic *Stand on Zanzibar*, won the Hugo Award for Best Novel in 1969, the British Science Fiction Award, and the Prix Apollo in France. Mr. Brunner lives in Somerset, England.